Dear Canada

THE DEATH OF MY COUNTRY

THE PLAINS OF ABRAHAM DIARY OF GENEVIÈVE AUBUCHON

BY MAXINE TROTTIER

Scholastic Canada Ltd.

Québec, New France
avril 1759

Le 8 avril 1759

I have two names. The people here at the town of Québec know me as Mademoiselle Geneviève Aubuchon, for I was baptized so. However, the name given to me by my birth mother is *Miguen*, which means *feather*. I have been told that when my mother first felt me move inside her she saw a small blue bird fly across the sky. She chose my name in memory of that moment.

This is my journal.

Today, on the anniversary of my coming to Québec, I was presented with a lap desk by my foster mother, Madame Claire. All inlaid with mother of pearl, it is the finest gift I have ever received. Then I opened it. Inside was this journal covered in green leather, a silver inkpot, sealing wax, a dozen goose feathers for quills and a small silver penknife. There is also a brass *porte-crayon* and a set of leads for sketching or for writing when I am away from home. The journal is of a perfect size and fits in my pocket so that I may always have it and the *porte-crayon* with me. I was touched, but it was the seal that moved me the most, for Mme Claire had contrived to have it imprinted with my totem, a small bird.

I know that she wants the best for me, but the best means growing up French, something that disturbs Chegual deeply. To remember how important it is for me to remain Alnanbal in my heart — Abenaki, as the French call us — was very dear of her.

Le 9 avril 1759

But what to write? I asked Mère Esther just that question when I went to help at the Ursuline school this afternoon.

"Everything," she told me. "You are a well-educated girl of twelve years, Geneviève, taught by we sisters. Tell the story of your life."

I protested that my life is so quiet and ordinary.

She said that it is all the small and ordinary things that make up a good story, and that some day someone else might read my story. Mère Esther reminded me of all the letters and papers left behind by Mère Marie Guyart de l'Incarnation, the foundress of their convent here. Think of the stories *they* tell, she said.

Later, Mme Claire said much the same thing. No detail is too small. The ship's logs left behind by her poor drowned cousin, Capitaine Renaud? Read them, and one knows each and every adventure he and his men experienced. "You may think your life is ordinary, Geneviève," she finished. "If so, then bless that fact, for it may not last forever."

That made me shiver, for I knew exactly what she meant. We have talked about it many times, trying to prepare for what we hope will never happen. France and England have been at war for five years here and in other countries. Such horrible things have come to pass. The *Acadiens* forced from their lands. Our forts — Beauséjour, Frontenac, Duquesne, Carillon and even Fortress Louisbourg — falling into the hands of the British. There have been so many killed and so much suffering. It is only a matter of time until the British try to take our city.

I give thanks every day in my prayers that Québec is so well fortified and manned that the British cannot possibly succeed.

Le 10 avril 1759

So. I will try to set aside time each day for my story and begin where it is always best to do so — at the beginning.

I was but perhaps five years old — I am uncertain of my true age — when Chegual and I were found in our village by voyageurs, hard men who still had enough kindness within them to pity orphaned children. There had been an attack, with every living soul in the village killed or taken prisoner. All except for us, we two who had been wading in the river, we who had hidden in the reeds to watch and hear the horror of it all, we two who had crept back to mourn for days, surrounded by our dead.

The voyageurs brought us here to the city and we were taken in by Mme Claire Pastorel and her husband Monsieur Jacques Aubuchon, the surgeon apothecary. They had no children of their own. When I was seven years old, the year M. Jacques died, I began to attend school under the instruction of the Ursuline nuns. Chegual — who was given the name Joseph — was enrolled in the seminary school for young boys.

Such a thing did not suit him.

Where I took well to life here, he, being four years older, did not. Two summers ago when he and his friend Étienne L'Aubépine ran away to join the Abenaki people at the St. Francis mission, it nearly broke my heart.

"This is *your* way, Miguen," he said to me gently that morning. "I cannot live with the French as you do. Perhaps it is a good thing that you are like them now, but it can never be so for me."

He was correct, of course.

Le 11 avril 1759

Although my education at the hands of the Ursulines was completed several months ago, Mme Claire has seen to it that I continue my studies here. She sometimes speaks to me in English, but it is a difficult language at which I do not excel. French is my preference. As for Abenaki, I fear it is necessary that I speak it to myself each day so that I do not forget words.

My studies are no hardship. This house has the most wonderful library, and I spend time there when I wish. The books are marvellous. There are thirty-two of them, and that is not something of which many homes may boast. Among them is one precious volume of La Fontaine's *Fables*. There is *Lettres d'une Péruvienne*, by Mme de Graffigny. What a gossip she was! Mme de Graffigny would have been quite at home in the market, telling tales of other peoples' lives.

Some of the books I have been forbidden to touch. *Manon Lescaut*, for example. Madame says it is far too scandalous for a girl my age. She is correct, for once I peeked into it just to make certain her words were not an exaggeration, and it took an hour for my blushing to cease.

Le 13 avril 1759

What happiness!

Our Brigitte is to be married. It will be in the fall, naturally, after the harvest is in. Her fiancé, Pierre DesRoches, has a fine farm up the river toward Montréal. She will leave us once she is married, and no longer work as our housemaid, since her life will be with her husband.

Housemaids. Servants. What strange words to use about the women who are part of our family. Mme Babin we simply call Cook, for that is what she does so very well. The rest of us wonder how Cook never gains any weight no matter how much of her excellent food she consumes. I suppose it is because she is such a tall, thin woman. At least Brigitte's sister Madeleine will remain. Since they are twins, it will almost be like having Brigitte still with us. Only their laughs are different, Brigitte's being light and soft and Madeleine's hearty. Unlike Cook, they are very short girls, with small hands and feet. I have noticed that young men smile and wink at them when we are at Mass. Some young men are very bold.

Yes, we have servants, but I do my share, just as I would have in an Abenaki village. I can remember working in the fields with my mother — how I miss her and my father sometimes — helping her when she scraped and tanned skins, stirring a pot of corn and beans. The work was different, but it was work all the same.

"You will be able to run your own household much better if you know how the work should be done," Mme Claire has said more than once. "And hopefully, you will be able to manage your servants." This she says with a twinkle in her eyes since she knows very well that Cook is ignoring her. And so I work and prepare myself for the day when I have my own home. Strange. Sometimes it seems as though I spend all my days getting ready for life to begin.

Le 14 avril 1759

I count happiness in many ways. There is the manner in which winter sunlight shines upon me through the windows of Notre-Dame-des-Victoires when I kneel during Mass, turning the walls golden and warming my chilled hands.

There is the sound of children's laughter in the streets. Warm bread at breakfast, the sweet voices of the nuns when they sing in their choir, all are like rosary beads slipping through my fingers, counting happiness the way I count my prayers.

Now I shall count it in a different fashion, for Abenaki warriors who came to Québec to trade have told me that my brother is coming home. I am so filled with joy at this, that I can scarcely hold a quill. Blotches!

Le 16 avril 1759

Mme Benoit's savage goose is nesting in our laundry. She — the goose, not Mme Benoit — likes the steamy warmth of the place. Cook says that Mme Benoit had best bring her goose home soon or find the beast turned into a *ragoût*.

Le 17 avril 1759

Today when Mme Benoit came to the house to fetch home her goose, she said that the price of bread has risen alarmingly yet again. She expressed the opinion that we would be wise to hoard our food since war will surely come here to Québec. With the poor harvests of the last years and lack of supplies from France, life is certain to become a hardship.

Surely she is wrong about the last.

I will not think of such things and let them spoil my happiness. Only Chegual's return is important.

Le 19 avril 1759

Mme Claire and I went to the Ursuline monastery today. It is always a pleasure to do so. I enjoy seeing all of the sisters, but it is watching Mme Claire and Mère Esther together that brings me the most happiness.

They could not be more different; Mme Claire so short and a little plump, which suits her. Mère Esther so tall and slender — which I suppose suits her as well, as she has at least twice Mme Claire's thirty years. At least I think it is thirty — she will not confess her age to anyone! For such close friends they have many differences. Madame is sophisticated and influential here in the city, and she has even travelled in the New England colonies. She loves to read and learn about all manner of things. Mère Esther's world is that of God, the Church and the Ursulines. Where madame may go where she chooses, Mère Esther must remain within the walls of the monastery, since the

Ursulines are cloistered. Yet these women remain devoted friends, having known each other since Mme Claire herself studied at the school.

I have things in common with each of them, these two good women who have taken me into their hearts. What I share with Mme Claire is a hunger for books and learning and music. And a deep love of this town.

With Mère Esther I share a similar history, since she was taken by the Abenaki as a small child in a raid, living with them until Père Bigot ransomed her and brought her here. And as I was raised by Mme Claire, Mère Esther became the ward of the first Gouverneur Vaudreuil. It is said that when her family in New England learned of her whereabouts and begged her to return, she refused — even at the age of fifteen, she knew she was meant to serve God in Canada. Like me, she never saw her parents again.

They both have their feet planted solidly in the lives and worlds they have chosen. For myself, I am not always so certain.

Le 22 avril 1759

I was happy when I woke this morning, for the sun was shining, and since it is Sunday there would be little work to be done. I am not lazy, but neither am I a fool. I enjoy a day of rest very much, *merci*.

Now, though, my happiness could not be greater, for Chegual has finally returned after nearly half a year's absence. I cannot sleep, and so I will write down everything perfectly so as to give thanks to God for how He has blessed me. Mère Esther says work done well is a gift to God.

There I was, staring at the herbs in the tiny raised garden behind our house, longing to pull out a weed that had sprouted and knowing that I must not — it being Sunday, after all — when someone said, "*Kwai*, Miguen."

For a heartbeat I did not recognize him. His long black hair, so much like mine, was gone. Now he wore only a scalp lock, the rest of his head having been plucked clean. Fine blue tattoos ran across his face. More would be on his body and arms beneath the linen shirt he wore, I knew. For a moment I saw something in his eyes that mirrored my own thoughts. She has changed, he was surely thinking. I am wrong to have come here. But then I was in his arms, in the warm and loving arms of my brother, and I knew that neither of us had changed at all.

When Mme Claire found us, we were seated on

the ground, lost in conversation.

"*Kwai*, Chegual," she said, and spoke the words of greeting I have taught her. *"Toni kd'allowzin?"*

Mme Claire then insisted that he stay with us. The kitchen would be to his liking, she went on, for it was where he had always preferred to sleep in the past.

"My thanks, madame," he answered her.

I was grateful she had used the name Chegual and not Joseph — the Christian name forced upon him. He will tolerate *Joseph* from madame's lips, though sometimes when she uses it, he takes his *vengeance* by speaking to her as though she were a *habitant*'s wife rather than a lady. She does not care.

Later, much later, after Chegual and I had talked and talked and yet had only begun to say the things we needed to say, he gave me a gift, something he pulled all sleepy and limp from his hunting bag. It was a rabbit, not a wild rabbit with a white tail, but a small brown rabbit. One that had only three legs.

"She is called Wigwedi," he told me. How I laughed at that, for *wigwedi* is the Abenaki word for lynx. "A lynx took her front leg, you see. I saw her fighting for her life as bravely as a lynx itself." So he killed the lynx for its pelt, but thought that such a brave rabbit should live rather than go into his pot. I thanked him for bringing her to me.

The people here will see only a warrior hardened by battle. I, though, see his tender heart.

Le 24 avril 1759

I will give my rabbit the freedom of my room, for I do not mind cleaning up what she leaves behind. As for the rest of the house, I have promised that I will be vigilant. However, there will be times when she must be in a cage, as little as I like that. On the other hand, when left alone this morning when I went to Mass, she chewed the heel of one of my shoes! I scolded her for her naughtiness.

I decided to buy a cage woven of willow for Wigwedi. How Cook, Brigitte and Madeleine, all farm women, laughed at that. She will chew through the willow and be out in a flash, Cook said, adding that it must be made of metal or heavy wood. Then she snapped her fingers and said, "M. Ste-Anne, the *forgeron* — you must go to the blacksmith shop and ask him to make you a little cage."

With Wigwedi shut in my room, I did exactly that. The cage will be ready tomorrow.

Le 25 avril 1759

Strangely, Wigwedi, who is a friendly little thing, was quite the opposite when I returned with her cage today. I have learned something about her. The rabbit is a vengeful creature. And a patient one. She bided her time before she showed me what she thought of being scolded for nibbling my belongings.

Why is my pillow wet? I wondered this afternoon. Even if I had left my window open, it hadn't been raining. Was the roof leaking? Then I looked more closely at the wetness. It was yellow.

I picked up the pillow and sniffed it, just as Madeleine was coming in with a basket of clean linen.

"It is not the roof that is leaking; it is your *lapin*. Rabbit urine," she laughed. "She has fouled your nest, it seems, Geneviève."

You are a bad rabbit, I wanted to say as I removed the pillow covering. A very naughty rabbit, and perhaps Chegual should have eaten you. But I did not say any such thing. I have become fond of her, after all. Besides, it might have been worse. He could have brought me a moose.

Le 26 avril 1759

It seems that Chegual did not return to the town alone. That fact I learned this morning as I worked in the herb garden. There I was, bent over with a watering can in my hands, giving the plants a drink, when someone said, "*Salut*, Geneviève."

Salut, was it? Not *bonjour?* I was not certain I wished to make the acquaintance of such a brazen fellow, so I did not turn around at once.

But then he said plaintively, "Come now, Geneviève, surely you do not still bear a grudge against me? It was only a small piece of ice, after all. Surely such a thing could not come between old friends."

Only one person would have known about the ice dropped down the back of my *chemise* long ago. I turned then. It was Étienne, of course, with Chegual standing beside him.

Old friends, were we? Not only had he dropped the ice into my clothing, he had stood there grinning, knowing perfectly well I could do nothing since we were at Christmas Mass. I tried to keep my voice stern and my expression cross, but I could not. Étienne's smile has always been one that makes other people return it.

Welcome home, I said then, as lightly as I could, for he was staring so. If Chegual had not been there I would have been somewhat uncomfortable. It was Chegual whose words made the discomfort evaporate. If we *must* gape at each other, he told us, we could close our mouths so that insects would not get in. We laughed then and we were but two friends who had not seen each other for a long while.

Now though, alone in the quiet of my room, I have had time to turn over in my mind what I have learned today. When Chegual left Québec, he wished only to return to our people. Étienne though, having no family to keep him here, sought adventure.

He certainly found it when he was adopted by the Abenaki, for like Chegual he is now a warrior. In truth, except for his dark blond hair and blue eyes, one could think him Abenaki. If he had remained here, it would be his duty to fight with the militia should the British attack, since he is more than sixteen years of age and required to serve. Instead, Étienne is an ally to the French, along with the other warriors. When I told him that was very confusing, he simply laughed and said he saw it as a simple thing.

"I will make my life in both worlds, Geneviève.

I am no hero, but I will die before I live my life under the yoke of the British."

Plus tard

They are all asleep or at least in their beds — Mme Claire down the hall from me on the second floor, Brigitte and Madeleine together in their room on the third floor, Cook in her room next to theirs, Chegual and Étienne in the kitchen. Only Wigwedi and I remain awake, she washing her face with her paw, me writing, having already washed my face. With warm water and a soft cloth, not with my paws.

Prayer has not set my mind at ease, nor has pacing my room. All I can think of is the war, something that Étienne's words brought sharply home. He said that he was no hero, but it was not that. It was —

Plus tard encore

How he could have heard me walking, I have no idea, but Chegual did. I am glad of it. He came up and whispered that I must let him in. Then we sat and talked. Not of death, although he had seen how Étienne's words had disturbed me. Rather we talked of the Abenaki village at the St. Francis mission, of his and Étienne's happiness there, and of Wigwedi, who was asleep in her cage. How I love my brother. When we speak of such things, when I see how proud he is to be Abenaki, the same pride rises in my heart. I wish that our parents could see the young warrior standing before me.

Le 28 avril 1759

Chegual told me the strangest thing this morning. He said it with no more concern than if he had been discussing the weather.

"He says you have grown up," he began. When I asked who had said such a thing, Chegual answered, "Jigenaz," using Étienne's Abenaki name. My brother looked at me long and hard, studying my face. Then he shrugged his shoulders. "He says you are comely. I myself cannot see it."

How I blushed.

I thought about this all day, although I tried not to do so, since vanity is unbecoming. Finally, I examined my face in a mirror. Our home has mirrors of all description that reflect the light and make the rooms seem warmer and larger. I am accustomed to seeing myself as I pass by them, and think little of it.

Tonight though, I examined my face carefully with the looking glass that I keep on my dressing table. I saw the familiar shape of my features, the tawny skin and dark eyes, my black hair ready to be braided for the night. It is not a white face or even a French one. It is an Abenaki face, something of which I have become very aware as the years have passed. It is a serviceable countenance with eyes that see well, ears that work properly and white teeth for chewing food. But comely?

Perhaps Étienne has been out in the woods too long.

Le 29 avril 1759

Mme Claire has offered work to Étienne and Chegual. Until their skills as warriors are needed, they will be in her employ. Though I hope it is their work as interpreters, not as warriors, that will be called upon more often — both of them having Abenaki and French and the English they learned from captives. How I pray they will be safe.

Chegual declined. "Work?" he laughed. "Perhaps I will take charge of Étienne as he slaves for you, and I will go with him when he hunts. Only to make certain he does not become lost in the forest, you understand."

I know my brother. He will not let Étienne work alone.

Le 30 avril 1759

Mme Claire has decided that she prefers water from one of the wells in the Haute-Ville, the one at the Place d'Armes. There is a well here to the west of us in the Basse-Ville, but madame insists the water is not clear enough.

Cook rolls her eyes when she thinks madame cannot see her, which is seldom. "Salt cod poached in water from the well here is no better or worse than salt cod cooked in any other water. It is still cod."

"Nonsense," madame counters. She insists that Place d'Armes water is sweeter and more pure. "It is all that my dear husband used for his tinctures and I have decided that it is all I will have in this household."

So the water must be brought all the way down to our house in the Basse-Ville from the Haute-Ville, though the road between the two sections of the town is extremely steep. But Étienne solved the problem. He would rent a dog, he said.

Anything may be rented here in the town, from looms, to ovens to houses. Why not a dog?

Le 1er mai 1759

Étienne, to the unending amusement of Chegual, who could barely stand for laughing, rented an enormous beast called La Bave. She is called this because she drools a little. Mme Claire says that a little is enough, but I think La Bave is a fine creature. She is no ordinary Québec dog, being from a far-off island called Île de Terre Neuve or New Found Land. As black as ink, La Bave is tremendously strong and suited to the work she does, which is pulling a cart loaded with a cask.

I am to go along with them tomorrow and bring back water to fill the large copper cistern that stands in the kitchen. What fun that will be.

Le 2 mai 1759

Away we three went this morning, with Chegual behind me, down Sault-au-Matelot, right onto Des Soeurs, all the way up Côte de la Montagne. I held onto La Bave's harness, as did Étienne. When we reached the top of the hill, Étienne stopped the cart in front of the stately old Jacquin house so that La Bave could rest. Above the door of the house is a carving of a dog chewing a bone. There are words as well.

Je svis vn chien qvi ronge lo
en le rongeant je prend mon repos
vn tems viendra qvi nest pas venv
qve je morderay qvi mavra mordv

Étienne, wiping his forehead with the back of his hand, asked what it said. He lifted his shoulders and grinned at me. No matter how hard the good priests tried, they somehow never managed to teach him to read, he confessed.

And so I read it for them. It said:

I am a dog that gnaws his bone,
crouch and gnaw it all alone.
A time will come, which is not yet,
when I will bite him by whom I am bit.

Ha! Chegual laughed and he went on about how that is what they will do to the British if they come here. And he growled at me, which caused La Bave to cock her head at us, but she did not have long to stare, for Étienne was again urging her on.

We turned left onto Château and proceeded past the houses to Place d'Armes and the well. I was not surprised to see that others had come for water, and so we took our place in line. It might have been tiresome but for Chegual and Étienne, who commented in Abenaki on every woman and girl who passed by. I tried not to listen and definitely tried not to smile, but when Mme Prunier came into sight — she was wearing a gown the most dreadful shade of purple — and Étienne said something about a walking plum tree, I lost my resolve. I leaned over La Bave and made a pretense of scratching her as I tried to contain my laughter.

It was not until we were on our way back down the hill with Étienne singing a song about plums and prunes and grapes — one that he was inventing — that I began to laugh aloud.

For all that time today I did not think of the possibility of war.

Le 3 mai 1759

Having three legs does not stop Wigwedi from getting into mischief or from nibbling at the sprouting, tender herbs in my garden. It has not stopped her from nibbling the corner of this journal either, as I noticed last night. Books are a precious thing, but there is one in the library that years ago was left out in the rain. The pages are so blotched and warped that it is impossible to read.

When I took it from the shelf, Mme Claire asked what I could possibly think to do with such a disaster. It may as well go into the fire.

It is for Wigwedi, I told her, explaining that if she had a book of her own to chew on, she would likely leave mine alone.

How Mme Claire laughed at that. "An educated rabbit," she said, wiping her eyes with a lace-edged *mouchoir*. "Only you would think of such a thing, Geneviève."

Le 4 mai 1759

I have a small telescope, a brass one that collapses so that it fits in my pocket. Mme Claire gave it to me. Her cousin Capitaine Renaud was a privateer who took as plunder many interesting things from the British vessels he captured. Of them, my favourites are the telescopes.

When Capitaine Renaud's ship sank years ago and he drowned, his estate and possessions came to Mme Claire. His furnished house in the Haute-Ville on Rue St. Louis, one that has a beautiful hawthorn tree growing in its walled garden, madame has at times rented out, although at present it is uninhabited.

There is a larger cherrywood and brass telescope that stands on one of the tables in our library. But the finest — one made of brass and mahogany that stands on a tripod — is the tele-scope in the fourth-floor study. With it I can see to Île d'Orleans as well as across the river. And if the telescope is moved out onto the balcony, I can just see the beautiful waterfall, Chutes-Montmorency.

I pray I will only ever see beautiful things through the telescopes.

Le 5 mai 1759

Today is Saturday, and so I went to the market this morning in the company of Étienne. My list was not long, since Mme Claire's pantry and attic are still fairly well stocked. Sacks of flour, dried peas, oats and the corn that Chegual so enjoys, barrels of salted eel and pork. We will not starve. Still, there is often something we need and so I shop.

Today it was butter only. Madame does not keep a cow. Where would she put it if she could? Étienne says it could live in the parlour, which is a *drôle* thought.

Le 6 mai 1759

Since it was Sunday, and a day of rest, I could shamelessly read and play with Wigwedi today. Not at the same time, of course. Well, as much as she will play, for she is not a cat or dog, but a rabbit.

She is an odd little creature. When I scratch the floor in front of her, she will come to me and lower her head and body. Then she folds back her ears. She likes to have her head stroked and the bases of her ears scratched. At first I thought she did not, since she would grind her teeth. Now I believe it is a sign that she is enjoying my attentions.

Chegual caught me whispering to Wigwedi and said, "You have French and Abenaki, Geneviève, and a bit of English. Can you also speak rabbit?"

I answered with my nose in the air, "Well, of course."

Le 7 mai 1759

A great flock of *pigeons de passage* came to roost in the woods during the night. Cook says she has never seen them do this so late in the year. Hunters do not even shoot the birds. They are so thick in the trees that they may be knocked out with sticks and then their necks wrung.

Dishonourable, scoffed Étienne, as he and my brother loaded their muskets and prepared to hunt. They left immediately, since a migrating flock can disappear at any moment.

L'après midi

What are we to do with nineteen pigeons? Eat them, Chegual commanded. And salute the twentieth bird, for it escaped.

Le 8 mai 1759

There is now an encampment of Abenaki warriors outside the city.

Alnanbal. It means *men*. It seems to me, though, that the Abenaki are not treated as men, as equals to the French or even to the Canadians. The warriors may come into the town during the day, but unlike Chegual and Étienne, who were once residents of the town, they are required to return to their encampment at night.

I wondered if their companions dislike the fact that my brother and Étienne remain here. When I asked him, Chegual said that they understood. His duty was to protect me from what could happen when war came. And Étienne's — or rather Jigenaz's — place was with his friend.

"If we were to leave Québec, Miguen, that would not be necessary," my brother added. He talks of war and how the British will come, and that we must leave Québec before it is too late. He would have said more, I know this, but for the expression I could not keep from my face.

I am surprised it has taken him so long to begin arguing for our departure.

Le 9 mai 1759

I dreamed of my parents last night. When I woke, I could not keep myself from weeping. It does no good at all, for it cannot bring them back. I know I am loved by Mme Claire and Mère Esther, but still. I will always miss them.

Le 10 mai 1759

What excitement!

"A marvellous ship has arrived and is now at anchor in the basin. Mme Claire, surely you will permit Geneviève to see this spectacle from the edge of the river with her own eyes." Those were Étienne's exact words.

And these were madame's. "Yes, if she puts on a cap and remains in the company of you and her brother, who will both make certain she does not disgrace herself by running and falling in the street. And if I receive a full report."

I must leave.

Ce soir

The excitement has given way to other emotions.

We three walked until we were out of sight of the house. Then Étienne announced that we were proceeding far too slowly. We must run. "But I am not allowed to run!" I cried.

You are not to run and *fall*, he told me in a most reasonable tone. He and Chegual would make certain that I did not fall.

And so we ran madly down the street — how I love to run, although it is unseemly — toward Anse de la Canoterie with me between Étienne and Chegual, each of them holding tightly to one of my hands. It is a good distance from the house to the Canoterie, about 500 *toises*, and I was puffing a bit when we arrived to join the crowd.

I pulled the spyglass from my pocket and put the glass to my eye to more closely examine the vessel.

"She is a frigate."

That was said by M. LeBlanc, the merchant who hides what remains of the eye he lost in war with an eye patch. He was once the capitaine of his own ship, and although he is far too old to go to sea any more, he still has a keen interest in anything nautical.

It is called *Chézine*, I told him, still peering through the glass. And it looks new.

She, he informed me. A ship must be called *she*. He said that she is new, having been built at the shipyard at Nantes in France just last year. She has more than twenty guns, and is 115 *pieds du roi* long. A fine vessel, although not a ship of war, he called her. Just then two small boats were lowered down the side of the ship. Sailors climbed into them and took up oars while armed soldiers followed. Then a white-wigged officer — a gentleman, by the cut of his clothing — stepped down into one of the boats and seated himself. Louis-Antoine de Bougainville, someone whispered. Général Montcalm's *aide de camp*.

When the boat reached land, Sieur de Bougainville stepped ashore, his face unsmiling and serious. People called for news, but the soldiers had none to give. They formed a party behind and before the officer, shouting that we all must step aside, that Sieur de Bougainville had business with the Intendant. With not a word to anyone, away they went.

When I reported each detail — except for the running, of course — to Mme Claire, she shook her head and heaved a great sigh.

"No news for the people, is it?" she said. "That

is easily remedied." And she went to her desk, spread her skirts, sat, and said over her shoulder, "Geneviève, find Étienne." She was already writing as I hurried away.

Étienne arrived moments later. He had been splitting kindling behind the house.

Mme Claire folded the sheet of paper and handed it to him, saying that he would deliver it to the capitaine of the ship *Chézine*. The capitaine being Sieur Nicholas-Pierre Duclos-Guyot, an old friend of her dead husband's. He was to run. She gave me a piercing glance. It is impossible to keep secrets from her!

Then when Étienne had left the house she told me to go straight to my room. I could not help but droop a little, but I did deserve punishment for disobeying her. Then she smiled. "You will go straight to your room with Madeleine and pick out the finest of your gowns. She is to make certain there are no spots on it."

I was thoroughly confused.

"*Vite*, Geneviève!" she said with a laugh. "We are to have a dinner party."

Le 11 mai 1759

I again spent time at the monastery school today, helping the littlest of the boarding students, the *pensionnaires*, write letters home. There are always a great many ink blots and stained fingers during these sessions. It did give me a chance to visit briefly with Mère Esther and tell her of Mme Claire's plan. An answer had come early this morning. There is indeed going to be a dinner party tomorrow evening, and I am to attend it. My first true dinner party!

"Bien," said Mère Esther. "You are not a child any more, Geneviève, and it will be an excellent opportunity for you to practise conducting yourself in a ladylike manner in the presence of gentlemen. Do not disgrace us now." So many times she has told me that no matter how one lives life, no matter whether one is a nun or a married woman, a widow or a spinster, good manners are always important.

I am so excited that I can barely think clearly, much less remember my manners, but I will not disappoint her or Mme Claire.

Le 12 mai 1759

All is ready for the dinner, and so I am able to take a few moments to set down my thoughts here. Madeleine and I have laid out the clothing I am to wear this evening. "Is it sinful to take so much pleasure in fine clothing?" I once asked Mère Esther. After considering my question she told me that *not* to enjoy that with which *le bon Dieu* has blessed me would be worse. I should be thankful for what I had.

And so I am.

There is a *chemise* of the finest linen, edged with batiste ruffles at the neck and cuffs. The gown is raw silk the shade of moss, and my stockings are white cotton with blue ribbons to hold them up. No one will see the ribbons, naturally, but still, they are lovely. New silver buckles on my shoes. I will wear a small cap with a double ruffle and a length of the same blue ribbon tied around it. Earrings of white amber and a ring to match. A silver cross tied around my neck with blue ribbon and a *fichu* of cream silk tied about my shoulders for modesty's sake.

There is other, far simpler clothing, folded away in my chest, for I still have the garments I wore when we first came to Québec. Madame, in her wisdom, did not insist it be burned because it was so filthy after our ordeal. Instead, Cook washed it all and hung it in the sun to dry. Whenever I touch the plain shirt, leggings and skirt, I can see my mother, seated outside our lodge as she made them for me. What would she think if she could see me dressed as I am now?

But enough of such rambling, especially when the memories can bring sadness. Cook is calling.

Tard

Always confused feelings these days. I am sleepless yet again. I have said my rosary and prayed for peace of mind, but it eludes me and so I have lit a candle and write.

The dinner party was a great success. The capitaine is a dashing man of perhaps forty-five years. He said I was to call him Capitaine Guyot. He came accompanied by two of his young officers, Marc Dubois and Louis Benoit, who were equally dashing in the manner of sailors. I fear I was rather overwhelmed by all this and could scarcely think of anything to say, and rather than embarrass myself, I said nothing.

But I curtsied properly. I had practised in my room. Madeleine had played the part of a gentleman and bowed to me, both of us laughing. And I did not spill food or my cider, so I was satisfied.

Until the dinner ended, that is, and the last of the dishes were cleared away.

Mme Claire gave the capitaine and his officers permission to light their pipes. It is illegal to smoke within the city for fear of fire, but this is a private home after all.

"Now," said Mme Claire. "Tell me what you know, monsieur."

He drew on his pipe, blew the smoke into the air and began. I did not listen closely. It was far more entertaining to watch Madeleine, who was peeking around the doorway making eyes at the young officers. This caused them to wiggle their eyebrows in what I suppose was an enticing manner.

Then I heard it. *War.*

"The supply ships are not far behind us, madame," the capitaine said, "but behind them is the British Navy." It seems that that is why Sieur de Bougainville went directly to Intendant Bigot, and it is also why he will leave Québec shortly to carry letters to Général Montcalm in Montréal.

The capitaine looked away then and it seemed to me that his voice could not have grown more serious, but it did and I shall never forget his words. "I fear that France has abandoned us."

Le 13 mai 1759

Our entire household went to Mass this morning at the Ursuline chapel to pray for the delivery of Québec from the British. Even Étienne accompanied us, although Chegual would not, the Catholic faith meaning nothing to him. Afterward, Mme Claire spoke at length privately with Mère Esther while we waited in the street. What things were being said! "The British are animals. Unbaptized *barbares!*" cried one woman. Her sister was at Louisbourg when it was taken last year, she went on. She said that if the king will not do more than he has, we would meet the same fate as they — deportation, starvation. "Eating grass like the cattle they will treat us as." People nodded in agreement.

Later, Étienne told me not to listen to them. They were fools. The city was a stronghold that the British would never be able to breach. Besides, with such brave men as they — he then elbowed Chegual in the ribs — the British stood no chance. Chegual laughed at his joking, but his eyes were not amused at all.

Tard

I knew it would come to this. It was only a matter of time before Chegual would truly press me.

"We must leave this place," he said when we walked alone by the river this evening. He would take me from Québec and back to the Abenaki mission at St. Francis so that I would be safe.

When I insisted that we were safe here, that the city is well fortified, he made a rude noise. He has heard stories of the British army, of its size and strength. He knew what the capitaine of the ship had said, that France had abandoned its people here. "I will not abandon you, Miguen," he told me. "I am your brother and your only living kin. The blood of our parents flows in both our veins, and you will obey me."

He knows how it moves me when he uses my Abenaki name. And what he says about France may be true. "But what of Mme Claire and Mère Esther?" I asked him. "I do not share their blood, but how can I abandon them after what they have done for me? For us?"

His answer turned my blood to ice.

"Then you may be choosing death, sister. If that is so, I will die with you."

Words only. I know that, but alone in my room they have come to life.

Le 14 mai 1759

They have slowly unloaded the supplies carried by the *Chézine*. 300 barrels of flour, 200 of salt pork, bales of blankets, rolls of fabric. And 4 muskets. Only 4! 145 barrels of brandy, of course, for Mme Claire says the officers cannot function without *eau de vie*.

Le 17 mai 1759

Nine more French ships have arrived. Perhaps France has not abandoned us after all. Of them, the *Maréchal de Senneterre* is the most spectacular. She carries 24 cannons, I have heard. Surely the British cannot possibly compete with our vessels.

I would ask Capitaine Guyot, but I am not certain I want his answer.

Le 20 mai 1759

We are to have an adventure, for Capitaine Guyot has extended an invitation to dine tonight with him and his officers upon his ship. I have once again been ordered to my room and my wardrobe.

Le 21 mai 1759

I have seen my first parrot and ruined my best gown. It was the parrot that ruined the gown, not me, and even Mme Claire can only be so cross with a parrot.

The dinner was an elegant one with a table set in what Capitaine Guyot called the great cabin. A servant stood behind each of our chairs, and with seven people dining it was a bit crowded. Much fuss was made of Mme Claire and me. She did look lovely in her blue silk gown. There are no women permitted aboard the ship as a rule, and so many curious glances — curious, but polite — came our way.

Capitaine Guyot began with an apology. He had been weary, he said, weary and under strain. He now insisted that of course France had not abandoned us at all. That the king and God would protect the people of this city. That with such wise and experienced men as Général Montcalm, Gouverneur Vaudreuil and Intendant Bigot — at that name he almost rolled his eyes — Québec was invincible. That said, conversation turned to other more cheerful matters.

We were introduced to M. Lavaseur, the ship's pilot, and to M. Raymond, the ship's physician.

Marc and Louis — they are so friendly it seems odd to refer to them as officers — were there as well. They introduced me to the ship's cat, Bernard, a huge sleepy creature stretched out in a square of sunlight.

It seemed that the ship's cook had been in the employ of a country gentleman and when the capitaine discovered this, had kept him busy since. The meal the cook had prepared was a tasty dish of poached cod in a dill sauce, a sort of bread that Capitaine Guyot called toasted soft tack, and eggs with candied citron peel for dessert. Delicious!

Afterward, there was talk of France and of acquaintances common to both Mme Claire and Capitaine Guyot. M. Raymond gave his opinions on the best way to treat scurvy and M. Lavaseur assured us that the British were such pathetic sailors and navigators that they would never make their way up the river to Québec. Each of their ships would run aground and that would be that.

Louis asked to be excused for a moment and left the great cabin. Capitaine Guyot was assuring Mme Claire and me that more supply ships were due to arrive, when Louis returned. He was not alone. Upon his shoulder sat an enormous grey bird.

"You will restrain that thing, monsieur. Mind

me now," said the capitaine firmly.

Mais oui! Louis promised that the parrot, Pitou, would be on his best behaviour.

What could it possibly do? I wondered. It was just a bird, after all. The conversation turned back to navigation, when Pitou decided that he liked the look of *my* shoulder and so he hopped onto it. He would not hurt me, I was assured. Then Pitou spoke to me. At length. And loudly. I have heard soldiers say such dreadful things, but never a bird.

Mme Claire's hand flew to her mouth, the men gasped in horror and Capitaine Guyot roared that Louis must remove the parrot immediately. Pitou, alas, did not wish to be anywhere but my shoulder and so he dug in his claws and said something even more foul. When Louis and Marc pried his claws from my gown, apologizing, their faces red, I fear that Pitou lost control of himself. He left behind a large green-white blob that stank horribly. As Louis carried him from the cabin, Pitou was singing a song. I will not set down the subject of the song's words here.

Later, when I told Étienne, he roared with laughter and said that it could have been more scandalous. "The parrot only gave you *one* verse of that song. I believe there are ten!"

Le 22 mai 1759

We baked today. Unlike many people in Québec who must rent an oven or use the public ovens, we have our own. Two, in fact. When the weather becomes warmer, Étienne will take apart the sheet-metal stove and set it up behind the house, but for now it is cool enough for us to bake using the brick oven.

Cook has a special wooden trough into which she put the flour and about three pints of warm ale, with yeast and salt to season it. She kneaded it well, covered it with a cloth and set it aside to rise. Later I shaped the dough into round loaves and used the flat wooden paddle to put them into the oven and to remove them when they were done.

The smell of fresh bread. What comfort there is in such a simple thing.

Le 23 mai 1759

Général Montcalm returned to the city last night, Étienne has told us. Étienne seems to hear news sooner than anyone else. I will admit that his sources are perhaps not always the most *respectable*. Étienne favours the taverns now and again. He says they are an excellent source of information.

They are also an excellent source of beer, I suspect.

Le 25 mai 1759

It is happening. Signal fires were lit at midnight last night to alert Québec that the British are coming up the river. Their ships are at St. Barnabé! It is so close.

There has been a meeting. All the capitaines of the merchant ships and the French naval ships were in attendance. The crews of these ships — 300 men — are now digging an entrenchment along the east bank of the St. Charles River. The soldiers will fight from their positions behind it. Other men have been sent out to Montréal and Trois Rivières to bring back the soldiers who wintered there.

I thank *le bon Dieu* that we will be so well equipped should the worst happen.

Le 26 mai 1759

People are beginning to leave the city, but Mme Claire refuses to leave our home, her faith being in the strength of our military and the town. Brigitte is gone, taken by her fiancé to his family's farm up the river, he like many others having responded to

Général Montcalm's orders. Women, children and even farm animals are to be hidden away deep in the forest. Our sailors will pull up the buoys and navigation marks along the river and then put in false ones to confuse the enemy and cause their ships to run aground.

The enemy. I have never thought of a single human being in such terms before in all my life.

Le 27 mai 1759

What a fearful thing is being done! Five of the largest ships as well as three small ones are being converted into something Capitaine Guyot calls fire ships. He explained that they will be set afire when the moment is right, and they will be sailed into the British fleet so that their ships burn.

I can barely imagine the horror of this. It is not only the ships that will burn.

Le 30 mai 1759

I walked to the Haute-Ville this morning to take a note to Mère Esther from Mme Claire. She told me the contents, knowing my natural curiosity.

"I would like to visit with her tomorrow," she explained. "To spend time with an old friend would cheer me, I think."

I can recall how worried I felt as I walked up the hill. Worried for the possibility of war, but worried for Mme Claire who is so cheerful. That cheeriness is slipping away.

Le 31 mai 1759

We visited the monastery this afternoon, spending two hours with the good nuns during their recreation period. Mère Marie de la Nativité, being the Mother Superior, may receive visitors at other times — she must carry on the business of the monastery, after all. But apart from those duties, she and the nuns are cloistered, living under the strict rules of the Ursuline order, and so can see outsiders only at certain times.

It was a familiar scene. Groups of nuns sat here and there in the walled garden, or walked in pairs. There are forty-five women here. One would think that a convent is a serious place, and it often is, but not during recreation. Then it is the duty of the sisters to cheer each other in whatever way suits them best.

I had brought a tincture of mint I had made for Mère Angélique, who suffers from the toothache, and a large jug filled with willow-bark tea for those who have pains in their joints. Mère Jeryan and Mère Charlotte are surely both afflicted with this, although they do not complain.

"*Le bon Dieu* watches over us, Geneviève," Mère Charlotte always says.

"There is nothing to fear from death," Mère Jeryan always adds.

Mère Esther and Mme Claire discussed the possibility of war. There was nothing to be done, they both agreed. Nothing, except to pray for our own deliverance. And pray for the British.

"Yes," said Mère Esther, speaking to me as she caught my expression. "You must pray for them and for the militia from the British colonies who will surely be with them. There is good in all people, Geneviève."

I have thought about what Mère Esther has said. If there is good in the British and their allies, then why did they besiege and take Louisbourg? Why did they seize the farms of the *Acadien* people and send them into exile? And why do they think to attack Québec?

But I have prayed for them tonight. They are animals and know no better, I suppose.

Le 1er juin 1759

I have learned the *real* reason for yesterday's visit. Mme Claire wished to seek Mère Esther's advice regarding me. They make me feel as though I am still a child at times, but still I am grateful for their love.

It was Chegual who began it, wanting me to go to the Abenaki encampment just beyond the city. He has taken to visiting our people each evening. There is sickness there, it seems. Not smallpox or ship's fever or griping in the bowels. It seems that there are children in the camp and some have sore eyes and no surgeon in the city will help them.

Mme Claire told me the outcome of her discussion with Mère Esther. I am not to visit the Abenaki camp at night. Neither Mère Esther nor Mme Claire consider that to be appropriate. But I may go tomorrow during the afternoon if both Étienne and Chegual are with me. Then she grumbled, "For shame, that no one will minister to little children."

Tard

At first I thought that I would not write of my visit to the encampment. It disturbed me so. But in the end I think it might help clear my mind.

At Cheǵual's direction I dressed in my plainest, oldest clothing. We set out walking through the Basse-Ville and up the hill, I carrying a covered basket. Both he and Étienne carried muskets and had tomahawks and knives at their waists and sheathed knives hanging about their necks.

At first I thought little of that, but then it occurred to me that they seldom go about armed when around the house. Will there be danger? I wanted to know.

None, Cheǵual assured me. Not if he was with me.

"It is only that we will be in the presence of warriors and must appear to be warriors ourselves," said Étienne. He made a horrible face. "Fearsome warriors."

We left the city and set out northeast across the Heights of Abraham, across the open sunny fields toward the woods. It was cool within, since the leaves on the trees have not achieved their full growth, but the coolness was pleasant. If I had been alone, I surely would have been lost, but Cheǵual knew the way.

Then, there it was. The Abenaki camp.

There were nearly a thousand Abenaki there and more people of other tribes camped in the woods. Some of the warriors had set up lean-tos of canvas to shelter their families, although I could not conceive of why a warrior would bring his women or children into the danger of war. When I said so to Chegual, he was silent a moment before he spoke.

"Because they do not wish to be separated from them, Geneviève," he said gently. "Because they would rather die together than be apart."

The people's eyes followed us as we made our way through the camp. Some of the men were reclining before their lean-tos. Some were eating, others were cleaning their muskets or making ammunition with molds and bars of lead. When one of the young warriors called out to Chegual, my brother tossed an answer over his shoulder and the man laughed. So did Chegual and Étienne. I did not. I was not amused to hear him asking if I was for sale.

Then we stopped where a woman sat on a woven mat — an *anhahkoganal*, as we call it — made of cattail rushes. There were two children, a boy of perhaps twelve years and a girl who seemed a bit younger. The eyes of the girl were sore and crusted with matter.

"This is my sister. She is a healer," Chegual explained. The woman's husband was his friend, I learned, as I knelt on the mat and uncovered my basket. I took out a stoppered bottle and a soft cloth. I explained to the girl in Abenaki that it was but a wash of goldenseal roots, and that it would soothe and heal her eyes if she bathed them with it each morning and night. I watched as she did this for herself and smiled when she shyly thanked me. Then I went to three more families where I offered the bottles and cloths to those with sore eyes.

Now that I turn it all over in my thoughts, I know that it was not the simple way in which the people lived that disturbed me. Nor was it the sickness I had seen. It was that Chegual seemed so much a part of the encampment, so at home there, as did Étienne. I, who am Abenaki, did not. Even the way the Abenaki words sounded as they came from my lips was not quite right.

It makes me wonder who I am.

Le 2 juin 1759

I have heard at the market that our soldiers have taken a deserter, one from the colonies. He has been brought to the Dauphine Barracks, where he will be questioned. What sort of man abandons his own country and its cause?

Plus tard

I have spoken to the deserter. I suppose I should cross out that last, having written it in my excitement, but I want this journal to remain tidy, so there it stands. It is only a small exaggeration. I did not speak to the deserter, whose name is George. His last name is an unpronounceable English one. It was Étienne who talked with him as this George passed by the house.

"So now he will fight alongside those who were once his enemy," Étienne told me, shaking his head. "What a thing that is, eh, Geneviève?"

What a thing indeed.

Le 3 juin 1759

Today is Sunday, and so we went to Mass at Notre-Dame-des-Victoires. Everyone knows that merchants and artisans may not sell their food or wares on the steps of Québec's churches. But today, as we left the church, there was a boy standing on the steps holding a basket. In the basket was an eel. I knew exactly what would happen and I was not disappointed.

"Be gone!" called a passing soldier, a white-coated one, scolding that the boy knew the law. The boy ran off, but not before exchanging a wink with Cook. When we returned home the boy was waiting with his father at the kitchen door, their hats in their hands, a bucket of live eels at their feet. It may be against the law to sell eels at the church and perhaps it is a sin — a small sin — to purchase them on a Sunday, but still, Cook did so.

"It would be a worse sin to pass up such an opportunity," she told me.

The *tarte* she made with them was delicious, so I agree.

Le 4 juin 1759

Manure.

It is difficult to avoid, since so many pigs wander the streets freely. Some landlords will not permit tenants to keep pigs or even chickens, but it does not seem to matter, since many people do as they wish. There are no fences and so the pigs come and go quite freely. These pigs may be caught and killed by anyone who wants to do so. We, of course, do not engage in such practices.

Yet, it was tempting this morning when I opened the front door, only to see a very large sow reclining at the foot of our steps. I flapped my apron at it. Still it lay there. I told it to go away. Nothing.

Then I fetched a broom from the kitchen. By this time Étienne, who had been weeding in the herb garden, came around the corner of the house and stood leaning against the wall with his arms crossed.

"Will you sweep it away, Geneviève?" he asked, stepping forward and giving the sow a very firm nudge with the toe of his moccasin.

She rose to her feet, gave Étienne an evil glare, and trotted off. But not before she left her foul-smelling visiting card. Étienne laughed so hard he wept, but he was finally able to control himself well enough to get a shovel.

"Merci, madame *cochon!*" he called after her. "You have contributed to the richness of Geneviève's herb garden. Call upon us any time!"

I laughed at that. Étienne. He can always make me laugh.

Plus tard

Étienne has been called to duty with others of the militia. Chegual is going with him.

Le 5 juin 1759

I fear that I shamed myself when I bid them farewell, for I wept a little.

"Ah, Chegual," said Étienne, "these are tears of joy! Tears of relief that she need no longer listen to us teasing her." I laughed through my tears.

"It is only the British in their leaky ships," Chegual said, adding that one might as well fight women.

"Unless they are ones such as your sister," said Étienne, and I laughed again.

I watched them walk down the street, well armed, their muskets cradled in their arms. Étienne was singing *"C'est le Général de Flip,"* an old song that pays homage to the resistance of Québec when the town was under siege almost a century ago. When I went back into the house, my eyes were dry.

I have decided that the best way to keep from worrying until they return is to keep busy. Hopefully it will help, and I am grateful for Étienne's words. But if the British ships leak, it cannot be much, since they have successfully crossed an ocean. And what does it matter how the British soldiers fight? A ball from a cannon or a musket does the same damage no matter who fires it.

Le 7 juin 1759

Our small herb garden is nearly the only one here in the Basse-Ville, since there is really no room at all for gardens. Mme owns a large garden plot at the edge of the Haute-Ville — her *potager* — land where our kitchen garden is planted. Turnips, peas, cabbages, beans, onions, beets, peppers, cucumbers, garlic and endive. She often sends me there for seasoning herbs as well, savory for her soups, chives and basil for the salads.

The garden here at the house though is a very different sort of thing, for it belonged to Mme Claire's husband — may his soul rest in peace — so it is the garden of an apothecary with such healing herbs as elecampane, chamomile, chicory and angelica, soapwort, rhubarb, hops, valerian, mallow and comfrey. Each winter they sleep in their raised garden beds, covered in mulch, protected against the harsh weather, but now all are growing well. I use what grows here to make tinctures and salves for healing.

I have set out flower pots of lavender and feverfew on the windowsills. They are both beautiful and useful. I know I should be practical and think only of the good these herbs will do for those with headaches, but I cannot.

Somehow, these days, it seems so important to see beauty, given what is facing us.

Le 8 juin 1759

The hospital, the school, this house, Wigwedi. Such is the pattern of my days. There are fewer girls at the school now, since the parents of the *pensionnaires* have had them sent home. So many Québec families have left the town, taking their children with them. We have become a town of soldiers and militia.

Mme Claire will no more leave this house than the nuns will leave their convents. That I know.

Le 10 juin 1759

What joy!

Chegual and Étienne have returned, uninjured, and with four squirrels in their hunting bags, having the luck to spy the creatures as they went through the woods. Cook prepared a delicious stew with the meat, turnips and rice, all seasoned with fennel. Mme Claire would not let them tell a word of what happened until they had eaten. Then we sat in the kitchen — neither Étienne nor Chegual finding the other rooms suit them — and they began.

Some 16 *lieues* from Québec, the British ship called the *Princess Amelia* had anchored between Île aux Coudres and the shore. Our militia was to take prisoners, since some of the British were on the deserted island, all the people having fled. A group of men originally from Île aux Coudres went ashore and found two young British sailors riding an island horse. The fools were easily captured and brought back to the city, Étienne told us. I asked what would become of them.

Étienne only shrugged and laughed yet again, but I cannot chase his words from my mind: "What docs it matter? Torture, death, prison? They are British, after all."

Later Mme Claire knocked upon the door of my room. I could tell from her face that a lecture was coming. How correct I was: I am not to believe everything I hear about the British or their allies. Think of Mère Esther; think of *her* family, who surely are good people even if they are from the British colonies.

"You must judge each person one by one, Geneviève," she went on.

How shall I judge Étienne for his cruel words? Perhaps it is best not to judge at all.

Le 11 juin 1759

Mme Claire and I walked to Hôtel-Dieu today with pea soup for the sick. Étienne had rented the dog cart for us so as to make the work easier. I have become reasonably skilled at handling La Bave.

We saw the prisoners being marched down our street. They are only boys, younger than myself, what it seems the British call *midshipmen*. Young gentlemen officers. They did not resemble anything like gentlemen or officers, but rather frightened boys.

I think perhaps Mère Esther's advice is correct. I will pray for them.

What sort of war will this be if it comes here?

Pendant la nuit

I have argued with Chegual. Or he with me. I cannot say who shouted the loudest. I should feel ashamed of my behaviour, but he demands too much.

Plus tard

Better. We have spoken — spoken, not shouted — and my brother is resigned to the fact that I wish to remain here. We all make choices, I said to him. "Do you think I *want* you to fight the British?" I asked him. "I know you must, so I do not ask you to do otherwise and shame yourself." He nodded at that

But I know my brother. He has not finished with this yet.

Le 12 juin 1759

We walked to the meadow in the Heights today to gather up as much grass as possible so that I may dry it for food for Wigwedi. Our neighbour, Mme Volant, says that grass is the best food for rabbits. She knows this since she kept rabbits once. She still has a great fondness for them. With Étienne's help I was able to fill the dog cart.

Now the grass is drying in the sun and Étienne is also drying in the sun, having become soaked with sweat from the work. He did it all — scything the grass, bundling it. He would hear nothing of me even lifting a finger.

A single thing spoiled the afternoon once we were back at the house.

"You must be warm in those sleeves, Geneviève," he said at one point. Surely it would be permissible to untie the ribbons and go without my sleeves on such a hot day — who would see, here at the back of the house? I could roll the sleeves of my chemise as well.

Étienne is very forward. I could not control my blushes or my face. He is my friend and I know he did not mean to hurt me. Yet he did.

Le 13 juin 1759

Étienne has apologized. He did not know about my arms and why I would not go out in public with them bared. It seems he was unaware of my tattoos, which of course all Abenaki girls have. Perhaps he thought that since I was taken so young, I had none — not like other Abenaki girls my age, who would have their faces and legs marked by now, as well. I explained to him that only my arms have been tattooed with my totem, so that it is always with me. Holding my head high, I told him not to misunderstand — I am not ashamed of how I look or what I am. Rather, I am proud of it. I just do not like being the object of anyone's staring.

Étienne laughed at that and then said, "They stare often, I would suppose."

Yes, I admitted and I shrugged. I *am* different from other girls. I cannot help that.

He stopped laughing and I cannot say I entirely understood what he said next. "It is the difference at which they stare, Geneviève, but not in the way you seem to think."

Étienne. Bold and confusing.

Le 14 juin 1759

Poor Mme Delisle. She was very old, but still it is sad that she died in the night, mercifully passing away in her sleep. And just now I have learned that Mme Chesne, the midwife, attended the birth of Mme Thibodaux's baby daughter.

Life and death all in one day.

Plus tard

We went to the Abenaki camp this afternoon so I could see if my medicines had been of help. They had. One woman asked if I would accept a simple gift, and she put a bundle into my hands saying, "You are one of us."

It was Abenaki clothing. A plain linen shirt, woollen leggings, moccasins and a skirt.

When I returned home, I put it all on. How strange — and wonderful — it felt. It was almost as though I had returned to another time. My brother said that the clothing suited me. That it brought our mother to mind since I so resemble her. I let down my hair and stared at myself in the mirror. Was this how she would have looked? How I wish I could remember her face.

My mother always said that it does not matter what you look like on the outside. It only matters what you are on the inside. If I could see within myself, what would I find?

Le 15 juin 1759

Chegual and Étienne are gone yet again.

They did not offer to tell me where, or what they will be doing; perhaps that is just as well, for it would make me worry more. I made them swear to watch out for each other and to take great care. Chegual assured me that his skills as a warrior would serve him well and that he would guard Étienne, who is easily frightened.

Étienne, who normally would have also been teasing, only bowed to me. "No harm will come to your brother, Geneviève," he said solemnly.

Somehow that worried me more.

Le 17 juin 1759

What a glorious day for us! Our soldiers have captured a British ship!

We had heard muskets firing in the morning. Mme Claire and I went to the fourth floor and took turns peering through the telescope toward Île d'Orleans, but nothing could be seen but white smoke.

This evening we will go down to view the vessel.

Pendant la nuit

There is no ship, only a boat called a cutter from the warship the HMS *Squirrel*. What an odd name for a ship. Who but the British would name a ship after a rodent?

There are more prisoners, this time eight odd-looking men who were paraded through the streets under guard. They all had very long braids, some reaching nearly to the men's waists. And earrings!

Perhaps the British do fight like women.

Le 20 juin 1759

I have tried to imagine myself as a soldier. Could I ever kill anyone, even in my own defence?

Le 21 juin 1759

Chegual and Étienne. I am not certain when they will return, and so I lock the thoughts of them away, struggling against my fears. Fear, Mère Esther says, is sometimes a hard-fought battle, but like any battle, it can be won. I know nothing of battles, but I do know that today my bravery was sorely tried.

I worked at Hôtel-Dieu, as I do some afternoons, bathing the faces of the ill and holding the bowl for one of the surgeons, M. Laparre. I fear that I do not care much for him.

It is his eyes. They are so cold.

Mère Esther has often said that a person cannot like everyone, but that all should be loved as they are loved in the sight of God. I suppose that is true, but Mère Esther has never had to stand so close to M. Laparre and see the way those eyes of his shine when the blood begins to flow.

He had decided against leeches and had just opened the vein in Mme Joule's arm. The bowl — M. Laparre insists upon a deep bowl — was beginning to fill, when suddenly Jacques, the apothecary's boy, burst into the room, shouted and ran out again.

When I heard his words my own blood ran as

cold as river water. Mme Joule cried out and her arm jerked wildly, hitting the bowl hard. Her blood splashed out across the bed in a red fan.

"You careless girl!" shouted M. Laparre as he jumped back in vain. He went on about what I had done to his stockings, to his shoes and waistcoat! "What will I do without this waistcoat?" he raved. "It is my best." It seemed that his patients expected him to wear it. "It is a sign of my office, you stupid *indienne!*" he hissed.

His *waistcoat?* I had to fight to keep my voice even, battling my icy fear and the sudden colder anger that was beginning inside me. Did he not hear what Jacques had said? Surely he did.

What sort of sign will your precious waistcoat be against the British, M. Laparre? I wanted to shout back at him. Their warships have arrived and are up river.

Le 22 juin 1759

It is amazing how gossip runs through this town. It appears that Mme Joule sent a note to Mère Esther, who sent a note to Mme Claire, who in turn sent a note to M. Laparre, who has just now left our house having apologized to me.

It was a difficult apology to accept.

I am not stupid, so that insult meant little, but to have heard the word *indienne* come from his lips as though he were spitting out something distasteful? I accepted his apology. I will not forget what he said, though.

Le 23 juin 1759

I cannot help but imagine that the British will be filled with despair when they see the defences that they will meet. The town itself with its bastions and wall, the entrenchments along the river, with their redoubts and batteries, the camps of our brave soldiers.

Cook says the knocking together of British knees will be glorious.

Le 24 juin 1759

It was a horribly hot day with a fierce, blistering wind. Too hot to write.

Le 26 juin 1759

A dreadful storm in the night with much lightning and thunder that woke me many —

Plus tard

I heard shouting in the streets and the sound of the door being flung open. It was Chegual and Étienne and my relief was so great I could have wept. But then Étienne shouted that there were ships — British ships — sailing toward the town. Mme Claire, knowing my mind, immediately forbade me to leave the house and join the crowd of people who were hurrying to the river.

I raced up the stairs, taking them two at a time until I was on the fourth floor. By the time Mme Claire was in the room with me, my eye was at the large telescope.

I think I have never felt such dread in all my life. The British navy is here.

Le 27 juin 1759

I have counted them for myself. There are thirty-eight ships anchored off the south end of Île d'Orleans. All day today their boats went back and forth taking British soldiers ashore.

With the big telescope, I saw a party of men walk out of the forest and stand staring at our entrenchments, observing them with spyglasses. They were too far away for me to make out their faces clearly.

Then the strangest thing happened. One of the soldiers — a slight, red-headed man in the uniform of an officer — turned and looked toward Québec, his head raised and his hands on his hips. It gave me such a shock, for it seemed as though he looked right at me.

I know he could not see me, but still. I have looked upon a British officer and I sensed no sign of fear in him at all.

Le 29 juin 1759
L'après midi

I slept late today, as did Mme Claire, having been up most of the night, sick with worry over Chegual and Étienne, who had gone off suddenly. Have they been wounded? Has something worse come to pass? I cannot bear to think of any harm coming to either of them.

A neighbour pounded on our door some time past midnight. "The fire ships are burning," he cried. Mme Claire and I were both in our nightdresses, and so did not go out into the street, but rather to the fourth floor.

How horrible it looked with the ships burning on the dark river.

Très tard

Sleep eludes me. Worry keeps me awake. Chegual and Étienne are uninjured, for which I should give thanks, but I am more inclined to throttle them for what they have done.

They were aboard one of the fire ships last night! There was no danger, they told me, laughing as though it were some joke. The darkness hid them. Was I not proud of their daring?

"It was an adventure, Geneviève," Étienne said, laughing even more. "Besides, they asked for volunteers and we were willing. This time, anyway. *We* may choose our adventures, unlike the militia, who are subject to the military."

What other foolish things will they be willing to do?

Le 30 juin 1759

The sound of musket fire came from across the river this morning. I thank *le Bon Dieu* that both Chegual and Étienne are here at the house.

Ce soir

Five men of our militia have been taken prisoner. Seven were killed. Étienne had been at the tavern and learned of these terrible things from a man who had been lucky enough to escape.

"There is more, is there not?" asked Mme Claire, who was receiving his report.

Étienne did not answer at once. He glanced at me and muttered something about the rest not being fit for my ears.

Chegual said that he must tell me, that I needed to know what manner of men acted as allies to the British.

"Our dead men were scalped," Étienne said, scalped by men from the British colonies who call themselves Rangers. They are hard, hard men.

I am safe here in this house, but still I cannot stop thinking about what Étienne said. It frightens me. I am no innocent child. I know that some warriors take scalps and I have heard that the French and British do also, for the sake of revenge. It is a horrible practice, but one men are driven to in times of war.

I loathe it.

But what eats away at me is that Chegual is a warrior. What has he done in war? Has he taken scalps?

Le 1er juillet 1759

They say that the British Général Wolfe has sent out a manifesto, a proclamation, to the people whose farms are along the river. I saw this paper with my own eyes today in the market, for a man had torn it from the door of his parish church and brought it here. The *habitants* may return to their homes and if they remain quiet they will not be hurt. If they take up arms they could expect to suffer "everything most cruel that war offers." Those were the exact words.

What sort of man is this Wolfe if the thinks our brave men will not defend their homes and families?

Le 3 juillet 1759

Cook does not care to have Wigwedi underfoot in the kitchen. I have told her — Wigwedi, not Cook — that she must be a good rabbit and not interfere with the kitchen tasks. This advice sometimes goes into one rabbit ear and out the other with little effect.

This morning Cook was chopping cabbage and Wigwedi stood poised to grab at any bits that would fall to the floor. Fearful of stepping on my rabbit, Cook gave her a nudge with her shoe. It was a gentle nudge, but still it infuriated Wig-wedi. I have come to recognize the signs. She turned her ears backward, pressed them against her back and stuck her tail out stiffly. Then she growled.

Cook was not amused.

"Perhaps we should send Wigwedi out against the British," Madeleine suggested. "One insult and she would foul their nests."

Even Cook laughed at that.

Le 8 juillet 1759

Today at Mass I prayed that somehow the British might leave.

Le 9 juillet 1759

The British now have a camp downriver of Chutes-Montmorency. How can Montcalm and his soldiers have let such a thing happen?

Le 10 juillet 1759

Early this morning our garrison began firing upon the British camp. This continued all day until after the noon hour. The Basse-Ville was white with smoke and, in spite of the heat, Mme

Claire ordered all the shutters to be closed over the windows to keep out the stink. Again and again the cannons roared, fire spitting from the barrels. Only a tremendous thunderstorm caused them to stop.

Hail fell, bigger balls of ice than I have ever seen before. Madeleine and I gathered a bucket of them. Cook poured out cider, and we floated hailstones in the cups. It made a most refreshing drink.

Perhaps it was a foolish thing to do, but it did cheer us.

Le 11 juillet 1759

Chegual no longer tries to spare me the horrors of this war. I know he thinks that he will surely frighten me into leaving with him. This morning he told us that an unarmed man and his two young sons were taken prisoner by Rangers a few days ago. Abenaki warriors who were hidden in the woods saw it happen. It seems that the Rangers feared the boys' cries would draw the French. To prevent such a thing from happening, they slaughtered the children and their father.

Later this day Mme Claire and I walked to Hôtel-Dieu. While she visited with Mère Marie-

Charlotte, their superior, I went to the upper floor of the building with my small telescope. There I had the most excellent view of our French encampment. I know that the British and their Général Wolfe are on the other side of the river. Are the Rangers there as well? If they are, then I am happy that I cannot see them. These Rangers have given the word *barbare* a new and sickening meaning.

Ce soir

M. Garneau came to call this afternoon. I believe he has a romantic interest in Mme Claire, but I dare say nothing. She has vowed never to remarry and so regards him only as a pleasant acquaintance, even if he is one of Québec's most prosperous merchants.

But as to the visit. It seems that a party of merchants and tradesmen — with M. Garneau among them — has presented Gouverneur Vaudreuil with a petition. They said that the British force at Pointe Lévis must be taken out because their cannons are far too close. "We offered to raise a formidable *détachement* ourselves," he declared. "At first Vaudreuil strongly objected, but what could he do but agree in the end? It is our city after all."

I asked who would fight, and was told that any able man or boy was welcome.

Étienne, who had been shamelessly eavesdropping in the hallway, was shocked. Inexperienced men and untried boys against the British army?

I said nothing, only thought that they will not be untried for long if this foolishness comes to pass.

Le 12 juillet 1759

Many of the city's people went out to the Heights of Abraham last night. We watched the merchants' *détachement* — I have heard it is well over 1000 souls — march away, and I think I have never seen such a lonely sight. It is true that some regular soldiers volunteered and that there was a good sized group of *indien* allies, but as for the rest, it distresses me even now to write about them. There was every sort of age and class of male, many of whom had probably not used a musket in years.

The hardest to watch were the young boys, students from the Jesuit College. Someone made a joke, calling them the *Royal Syntax*.

I could not help myself. "Yes, they study, monsieur, but at least they have the courage to fight,"

I told him. The man had the good grace to stop his grinning.

Chegual and Étienne, who could not stand the thought of such innocents marching out, refused to take part in such a reckless thing. Instead, they came back with us to the house, where Chegual argued in earnest that I should leave the Basse-Ville with him.

Étienne agreed. He said that if we will not leave, then at least all of us must go into the Haute-Ville to madame's other house — we will be far safer there.

"This is my home and Geneviève's home, and we will not be driven from it! Nor will Cook or Madeleine," cried Mme Claire.

Now it terrifies me that we may not be alive to enjoy our home.

Étienne and my brother have gone to the St. Louis Bastion to watch the outcome of the battle. We will pack tonight, taking only what is necessary, and leave for the Haute-Ville in the morning.

Tard

It was a farce. Only the Abenakis and the other *indiens*, Chegual proudly told me, were able to maintain control of their people. Tonight at the Abenaki encampment, Chegual's companions told him how they had scouted right to the edge of the British camp. But when they returned to make their report that the enemy was there unsuspecting, panic had begun within the *détachement*. In the darkness, our civilians mistook each other for British and began firing among themselves.

"They retreated to the canoes," Étienne said in disgust. He added that he was certain Montcalm now knows what sort of ragged army he commands. Then he sighed and admitted that at least the French soldiers have a talent for defending their positions.

I suppose he must have seen the unease on all our faces. Mme Claire and Madeleine are no better at hiding this than I.

"Never fear, Geneviève," he laughed. "The walls of Québec and its bastions will keep out the British."

Chegual and Étienne have returned to the Abenaki encampment, leaving me alone with my thoughts. I wish I could believe the reassurances Étienne gave us.

Le 14 juillet 1759

How to begin? I have little heart for writing now, but my journal is one of the few things that was rescued, and so I must tell this.

Only hours after the decision had been made to leave the house last night, at perhaps eleven, the British began to attack the town. At first I was not certain of what was happening. I was in my chamber folding and packing clothing, when through the open window I saw a single flare rise into the night sky. Then flames shot out from what I now know were cannons. They were such small flames and on the other side of the river. Surely they would do little harm, I thought. Then I could hear the sound of bombs exploding and of screaming.

I ran downstairs. Cook had thrown open the door, and we could see that people were already racing through the streets. "They are shelling the Haute-Ville," a woman cried. "Run! Run!" I thought that surely we would be safer here, if it is the upper town that is their target, and at that moment it seemed as though that must be true. But then something huge hit the wall of our house and we all fell to the floor. We helped each other up, much shaken.

Chegual and Étienne arrived just then, or I think in our terror we might have stood there and let the house fall down around us. They led us outside, herding Cook and Madeleine ahead of them, Chegual holding tightly to my hand and Étienne assisting Mme Claire.

Then I remembered. I pulled away from my brother and began to run back to the house. Wigwedi! I could not leave her to be crushed to death! Chegual threw his arms around me, saying that he would not let me do such a mad thing. I beat at his chest and called him foul names and wept and shrieked but he simply dragged me onward.

I can recall Étienne telling him to take us to the Ursulines. We would be safe there and he would find us. "I will get your rabbit, Geneviève," he assured me and then disappeared into the crowd.

It was a nightmare.

The bombs and cannonballs rained down upon the town, some crashing into the biggest of the buildings, but others exploding into houses around us. Our army began returning the fire and French cannonballs were flying toward the enemy. When we reached the monastery, it was to find that the buildings there had been hit as well. Inside, all the sisters were kneeling in the chapel before the Blessed Sacrament, praying for deliverance.

Mme Claire and the others joined them, but I could not. Instead, I went to stand in the doorway by my brother's side as he watched for Étienne. I was sick with worry for him and sick with shame for the way I had treated Chegual. But then out of the darkness and the smoke we saw our friend striding down the street, the cage under his arm with Wigwedi safe inside it.

"I am wounded," he said. "I had to chase her through the entire house and then she bit me. She is an ungrateful rabbit." Then he pulled my journal and *porte-crayon* from where he had tucked them inside his shirt. "I knew you would want this as well," he said.

I wept again, but this time with relief, and when I thanked him, he said it had been his pleasure. Except for being bitten. And when I tried to apologize to Chegual, he shrugged his shoulders. "You were fighting to save something that is precious to you, as was I. I cannot fault either of us, my sister."

I cleansed Étienne's hand as well as I could and bound it with linen. All night we three sat outside the chapel, unable to sleep, listening to the sounds of war all around us. When morning came, Mère

Marie de la Nativité ordered that the monastery be evacuated. They would shelter at Hôtel-Dieu. She had a letter from the bishop giving the sisters permission to leave the cloister in just such an emergency. Ten of the sisters volunteered to stay behind. Poor Mère Charlotte and Mère Jeryan had to be supported all the way, both of them in such distress and both with pains in their left arms and in their chests.

The hospital was far enough away from the enemy that no shells could hit it, but it was packed full of hundreds of terrified refugees. Rather than add to the burden being borne by the nuns there, Mme Claire decided then that we would carry on to her other house. I embraced Mère Esther and she whispered, "Trust in God, Geneviève. He will protect you." I embraced my brother, who left with Étienne to join the Abenaki.

And so I am here, alone in this chamber which has been allocated to me. Wigwedi has stopped trembling in fear and is asleep in her cage. No sounds come from Mme Claire's room, or from the room off the kitchen that Cook and Madeleine now share. There is only the scratching of my *porte-crayon*.

And the sound of bombs falling on Québec.

Le 16 juillet 1759

A note came from Mère Esther. Mme Claire wept aloud as she read that Mère Charlotte and Mère Jeryan had both died at Hôtel-Dieu the night of the bombing and had been buried in the garden cemetery of the hospital.

The poor, poor sisters, to have died away from their home.

A flag of truce was raised by our French army today, so that a message could be sent to the British. It was made clear that we will never cease fighting or surrender. We will never give up Québec.

Le 17 juillet 1759

Chegual and Étienne have returned unharmed. They were part of a war party — how hard that is to write — of Abenaki warriors who took three British prisoners who are now in the custody of our French officers.

The British prisoners said that Wolfe's army has not more than nine or ten thousand men in it and that he will not try a frontal attack, Étienne told us as they ate in the kitchen.

"And might you believe *this?*" he went on, his mouth full of bread and cheese. "An old man and woman are bringing refreshments to the British daily. Traitors!" His table manners have never been courtly, but I was so pleased to see him that he could have stuffed the entire loaf in his mouth and I would not have cared.

I said they must be lies, and asked whether he expected the truth from the British.

The firing has slackened on both sides now, which makes it easier to think. What if those old people *are* giving aid to the enemy? They are traitors, but what sort of things must have happened to them that would let them give comfort to the British?

Le 18 juillet 1759

Étienne rented La Bave and her cart today to salvage what he and Chegual could from the house in the Basse-Ville. I was not permitted to accompany them. They returned with what unspoiled food they could find, some of our clothing and all but three of our precious books. I asked Chegual to bring my lap desk if he could find it.

It all reeked of smoke.

The house was still standing, Étienne told us, but the damage was bad. And the houses on each side had burned.

"A house may be rebuilt," Mme Claire said with

tears in her eyes. "But once a life is gone, it is gone forever. Thank *le bon Dieu* we have been spared."

I will try.

Le 19 juillet 1759

The British have been moving their ships up the river. Today our French sailors attacked some of them. I could see it all clearly as the British vessels *Diana, Sutherland* and *Squirrel*, along with what I now know are transports, made their way up the river. *Diana* must have run aground. They began to toss her cannons into the water to lighten her. I counted at least twenty splashes. Lying at the bottom of the river, those cannons will do Québec no more harm. How those splashes might have lightened my heart, but for a terrible thing.

A gibbet was erected upon the Royal Battery in the Basse-Ville today and two sentries were hung for failing to do their duty. Perhaps they did not do their duty, but the British are already killing our men. Why must Général Montcalm assist them?

Many people went to watch the execution, some even making an outing of it with meals and cold drinks in covered baskets. We did not. Death is a serious business, Mme Claire observed sadly, not a circus.

I know I should harden my heart to such things, for the city must be defended. But still, all I feel is pity for those two men.

Le 20 juillet 1759

The British ships are now in the river above Québec. I am so frightened I cannot think.

Le 22 juillet 1759

A flag of truce was flown by the British this morning. We learned later that if a boat containing British wounded were allowed to pass the city unharmed, then some of our people who had been taken prisoner would be returned to us. The British were true to their word and so mostly women — women! — were brought ashore at L'Anse aux Mères in the afternoon. Étienne, who was there, said that a boat of strangely dressed men also passed by, a boat carrying cattle and plunder. The men were laughing at their own cleverness, for our soldiers could do nothing, being under a flag of truce.

"Think of it," Étienne said with a laugh. "Men who wear skirts!"

These men sound worse than the animals they were carrying.

Le 23 juillet 1759

Our great cathedral in the Haute-Ville has burned, the fire starting before noon this morning. Smoke poured into the sky as everything — the carvings, the vestments, the statues — were destroyed.

Le 24 juillet 1759

The shelling is ceaseless.

Le 25 juillet 1759

More fires from the heated shot the British use. Last night the Basse-Ville burned. Can anything be left of our home there?

Le 26 juillet 1759

Do the British possess every cannonball and shell in the world? It seems they do, for they bomb the city endlessly. My poor Wigwedi. The shelling terrifies her. The louder the sound, the more violently her nose wiggles. I pray that Étienne is correct that our home here in the Haute-Ville is too far for those bombs to reach.

Le 28 juillet 1759

A great mass of rafts and small craft chained together came down the river. This *cajeux* got very close to the enemy before our soldiers set it afire, but to no avail. The British boats towed it aside.

How are we not to despair?

Le 31 juillet 1759

Terrible fighting today when the British launched boats from Île d'Orleans in an attempt to take our position at Chutes-Montmorency. The enemy's ships ran aground and our soldiers fired upon them from their entrenchments on the Heights. Only a tremendous thunderstorm ended the battle. Étienne, who was there with Chegual, said that the skirted soldiers fought courageously. When they retreated, he told us, they would not leave until every one of their men got safely across the river. "They are brave men," he laughed, "even though they wore skirts."

"*Les Écossais,*" said Mme Claire. "If they are wearing skirts, I believe those soldiers are Scots" — she spelled the word for my benefit — "not British."

"They fight like Abenaki," Chegual said then.

"The British with their lines of men?" — he made a vulgar noise — "I hope to fight these Scots face to face some day."

I said nothing, only tried to keep my expression from giving me away as I heard his words. It is only here that I can reveal those thoughts. I am so afraid for Étienne and Chegual. There are times when they almost seem to enjoy the fighting. Surely I am wrong.

Le 2 août 1759

White flags — the Bourbon flag of our King Louis XV — were hoisted on the entrenchments today and yesterday in celebration of our victory.

Le 3 août 1759

The Intendant has called for all able people to journey on foot to Batiscan to bring back supplies to the city. I would willingly have gone, but for Chegual's protests. The first step you take outside this town will be a step with me back to St. Francis, he has told me.

It shames me that we leave such work to others.

Le 5 août 1759

It seems there is a British capitaine who lies wounded at Hôtel-Dieu. Yet another flag of truce was shown by the British, who wished to send linen and bedding to this officer.

Linen and bedding!

I have heard it said that thousands of cannonballs and shells have showered down on our town since the British began this siege. The bombing has been constant and heavy today. Their flags of truce sicken me. If it were my choice, I believe that I would take that officer and his precious linen and bedding and —

Plus tard

I have walked around the outside of the house a dozen times trying to calm my mind. My mind is not much calmer, but my temper is somewhat cooled. Flags of truce, courtliness, the manners of the officers — it all revolts me. What sort of a war is this?

Le 6 août 1759

The oddest thing. Through the large telescope I saw the British bury a man in the sand so that only his head showed. Is there no end to the barbarity of these people?

Le 8 août 1759

The shelling has been long and cruel today. They say little is left of our beautiful market. I myself would not have the heart to view it. There are fires and the smoke has poured up and darkened the sky yet again. And there was a great explosion, one that was not a bomb. Brandy in a vault beneath the house of two merchants blew up!

Étienne said, "Now *that* was a terrible waste."

How he manages to keep his spirits so high is beyond me.

Le 9 août 1759

Notre-Dame-des-Victoires has burned. Mme Claire was married there. I was baptized and in time made my first Holy Communion there. To have lost that church . . . I know in my heart that it was only a building, but it seems somehow that God is turning his face from us.

Chegual and Étienne left the house early this morning, saying that we must not worry over them. They might as well have told me not to breathe.

Le 10 août 1759

The Basse-Ville is all but gone. The British shelling and the fires have finally destroyed it.

I sat alone in my room today and wept for our loss. Our house, the library, all the memories. At least the British will never touch my memories.

And there was smoke, so very much smoke, coming from the mainland beyond Île d'Orleans. There are only farms there. No batteries or entrenchments. It is the farms that the British are now burning. They wish to conquer this country and take this town. Why do they seek to *destroy* it as well?

Le 14 août 1759

Heavy, heavy rain.

Le 17 août 1759

A miracle has happened, and I thank God that He has given us this small happiness. We have an addition to our household.

This morning, through the kitchen window, I saw a man beating a dog. He was dragging the poor creature and cursing at it. It was La Bave, the cart dog! She was matted and thin and her hair was burned off in places, but it was La Bave.

I ran from the house screaming that the man must release her, that La Bave was not his dog.

He said that her owner is dead, that she is his now, and that he will do with her as he pleases. Then what he said made my blood run with ice. "You look well-fed, mademoiselle. You in this fine house have meat on your table every day, I would wager. Today I will have meat on mine."

I have never seen Cook run before.

She chased him down the street, the *bâton* with which she rolls out pastry in her hand. The vile man could run faster though, and he soon disappeared. Then Cook walked back to our house to our applause.

"*Mauvaise est la saison quand un chien mange l'autre,*" she said with a shake of her head.

I agreed. It is a sad day when some cur of a man would think to kill and eat such a poor creature as La Bave. How she lapped up the soup we gave her! She is sleeping near the stove, her coat brushed. Wigwedi is not certain what to make of La Bave, but with luck they will become friends.

Friendship. It means so much.

Le 19 août 1759

We have heard the most horrible thing. British soldiers — deserters — have said that Général Wolfe is offering a handsome prize for any *indien* captured by his men. Whether the warrior be alive or dead matters not.

I am ill with fear to my very soul.

Le 20 août 1759

We have taken to sleeping in the kitchen, all of us together on pallets. That way if the house is bombed we will be able to escape together.

It was odd, and yet it was reassuring. I have never shared quarters with anyone since I came to Québec from my village. Even Wigwedi seemed to take comfort in it, although I cannot say she cares much for La Bave drooling on her cage.

Le 21 août 1759

Yet another flag of truce. Général Wolfe sent money to the soldier who rescued the wounded British capitaine, but Gouverneur Vaudreuil has returned the coins. As though we may be bought!

Le 22 août 1759

Word has come that Fort Niagara has fallen to the British — last month, they say. Mme Claire says it is a very old fort and not at all protected the way Québec is. Those words bring me little consolation.

No word or sign from my brother or Étienne.

Le 23 août 1759

They say that the British capitaine has died and that Mère Marie-Charlotte wept at his passing. My eyes are dry. To weep for the British?

I will never shed a single tear for the men who are causing such suffering here.

Le 25 août 1759

I thank God and Ste. Geneviève and every other saint in heaven that Chegual and Étienne returned in the middle of the night. Their arrival took us by surprise. La Bave set up a dreadful commotion, Cook armed herself with her *bâton*, Madeleine had a broom and the noise rivaled that of the British bombs.

I should cross that out. I must not make light of such a dreadful thing. It is only that I am so very weary. Worry eats away at me. Perhaps if I can rest for an hour.

Plus tard

They were filthy and covered with cuts and scrapes. I could have wept over those wounds, but I would have dishonoured myself and their bravery. I dare not ask how they came by their injuries, and neither of them will talk of what they have done in these last days.

For that I am grateful.

Le 27 août 1759

A very windy day. How wonderful it would be if the wind blew every British ship back up the river to where they belong in England.

Foolishness, but pleasant foolishness.

Le 29 août 1759

I have prayed and paced and done all I can to calm myself, but my thoughts are disturbed. The Abenaki. Chegual and Étienne's small wounds are healing, but what of the wounds of the Abenaki warriors? Some have their wives to care for them, but most are alone. And what of the children?

When I asked Mme Claire and my brother if he would accompany me to the encampment, she refused. As did he. Too dangerous, they insisted.

I cannot quiet my mind.

Le 1er septembre 1759

Étienne. He always knows what to say. That you wished to go is enough, Geneviève, he told me. That you think of your people says much about your bravery.

I am not brave, only worried, but still his thoughtful words comforted me.

Le 2 septembre 1759

Could Sunday Mass this morning have been more joyful? Could the hymns have sounded sweeter? God has answered our prayers. The British are withdrawing from Montmorency!

Le 4 septembre 1759

We have only the simplest of meals now, such as pea or vegetable soup with only a bit of meat in it, and our bread has oats added. The wheat that arrived from Montréal's harvest goes to feed the army. What we have will need to last until the

British ships are driven away by winter.

I wish it would snow.

Le 6 septembre 1759

A terrible storm struck us last night. I prayed — it is wicked, but I care nothing for that any more — that the British ships would be sunk or damaged. My prayers went unheard.

Le 8 septembre 1759

More rain today and yesterday. Cook says that we may all float away soon. Dear Cook. She tries to cheer me. But how can I feel cheer when Chegual and Étienne have left yet once more? It is only to get news of what is happening, they said.

Lies.

Le 9 septembre 1759

The heat is terrible.

Le 10 septembre 1759

A letter written by a notary came for Madeleine today with wonderful news. Her sister has been wed. Madeleine, who like her sister Brigitte can neither read nor write, listened as Mme Claire read it to her. "They have heard of our sufferings and are praying for us," she told Madeleine.

I believe they should be praying for themselves, should the British take Québec.

Le 13 septembre 1759
Tôt

Chegual is here in the kitchen, and I doubt that he is asleep. We have argued yet again.

He pounded at the kitchen door some hours ago, pounded and shouted until the entire house was roused and Cook let him in. He came to say that I must leave with him *now*. "I am her brother," he said to Mme Claire. "You have no authority over her and she will come with me. The British army is on the Heights and it will be a slaughter."

We women, all in our nightdresses and shawls, stood there gaping at him like sheep. It was Mme Claire who broke the horrible spell, ordering that coffee be brewed and bread and cheese served up. She must hear his report properly and we all needed something in our stomachs.

Chegual would not touch the food and I, for fright, could not. The enemy had come ashore in boats, he told us. They had scaled the steep cliffs and their army was massing on the Heights, far more powerful than could be imagined. Étienne had seen as well, and had been sent by an officer to alert Montcalm at his camp on the other side of the St. Charles River.

"Then there is hope!" I cried. "Montcalm will defend the city."

"There is no hope," Chegual answered. There were too many British. He said in a low voice that he had seen what they did when they passed through a village. He would not have such a thing happen to me. I must come back with him to St. Francis.

Such a heavy silence hung in the kitchen. Mme Claire came and took my face in her hands. "It is your choice, *ma chère*," she said, and the words nearly broke my heart. Everyone left Chegual and I then. We argued, and slowly I felt myself weaken, weaken, weaken, until all the fight was gone from my spirit.

He is my brother. I have changed into the Abenaki clothing that was given to me. It will be more suitable for travelling. I will pack this journal and take Wigwedi. My future is with Chegual, and I have agreed to leave Québec, although I do not know how I can bear to tell madame —

Plus tard

They did not believe Étienne! It was hours until he was permitted to speak to Montcalm and even then the général did not order his men to return to Québec. There are French troops moving onto the Heights now — perhaps Montcalm gave the order at last, or perhaps it was another of his officers — and it will not be long before the battle begins.

"It is not our battle," said Chegual to this. "I will not fight again for the French. I am taking my sister from here."

Étienne looked from Chegual to me and then back to my brother. He said this was my home. "How can you take her from Québec and out into the wilderness to face a way of life she knows nothing about?"

"She *is* Abenaki! As are you!" shouted Chegual, adding that our place was with our people.

"She is Abenaki," Étienne shouted back, "but what of Mme Claire and Mère Esther and all the others she knows here? It is not only a matter of blood."

How those words will be with me forever.

Then he said the unspeakable. "Or are you a coward?"

I thought they would fight then, that Cheğual would not suffer such an insult, even from his closest friend. The very thought of it tore at my heart.

He said, "I am no coward."

"Then fight with us!" cried Étienne. "And if you will not fight for the French, fight for Geneviève, as I do."

He knows Cheğual perhaps better than I.

Étienne asked for a *souvenir* from me then, a keepsake to bring him luck. I gave him my cross, saying only that he must take care. He kissed my hand, something he has never done before.

Then I kissed my brother and held him in my arms. And so they left, after Étienne commanded Cook to prepare a meal for their triumphant return, after Cheğual made me swear to stay inside the safety of the house, after making me vow not to worry.

How many promises will I break this day?

Tard le soir

I could say that there was a battle and that we were victorious, that there was cheering in the streets and that the British fled in despair. It would all be lies. There *was* a battle today, a terrible battle. And we lost. It is *I* who must call upon my will not to give up hope.

I broke my promises and left the house. Mme Claire tried to stop me, as did Cook and Madeleine, but I would not listen to their begging. I ran all the way to the St. Louis Gate, out of the town and down the road to the edge of the woods. Behind me I heard the roll of drums and the deep cheers of our soldiers as they began to march forward. I stood as they passed by me, the flags rippling in the breeze, our soldiers' white uniforms and the straight backs of our militia who marched with them, and I remember how my heart lifted and how I knew we would be victorious. How could such a gallant army fail Québec?

Someone called to me to go home, to take shelter in the town, that I was in danger here and I must go back. I did not. Instead I followed them, stopping at the edge of the woods. From behind a large maple — I dared not step out into the open — I watched our soldiers march toward where the British must be waiting, watched until I could no longer see them. There was the sound of musket fire. Screaming. White smoke rose into the sky. Cannons boomed out.

Then it happened.

It sounded as though an entire army fired at

once. I remember that I put my hands over my ears, but I could hear it echoing still. I prayed that it had been our soldiers who fired that volley, for if it was not . . . If it had been the British . . .

I ran back through the woods, sick to my very heart and filled with such fear for Chegual and Étienne that I could not stop from weeping. All those men, good men and boys. The screaming. I will never be able to forget that.

I could barely see the streets as I went through the town, back to the house where Mme Claire and the others would be on their knees in prayer. Wiping my eyes, I entered the kitchen, and saw that I was wrong.

"What has happened?" Madeleine asked me. "Is it over?" She was tearing linen cloth into strips for bandages. Mme Claire was rolling them and Cook was packing a basket of food.

Nothing short of a miracle could save us now, I told her.

"Go to the front door," Mme Claire said to me. "Watch for where they are taking the wounded."

We did not have to wait long. Soldiers appeared, some carrying unconscious men, others helping those who could just manage to walk on their own, and some bearing dead companions. The screams of those in pain were terrible. We followed to Hôtel-Dieu, and all the while I searched the faces of the wounded, praying I would not see Étienne or Chegual.

Some of the sisters were weeping over brothers or fathers who were dead or near death. Père Resche prayed with one man, then another. The smell of battle, of smoke and blood and sweat were everywhere.

Mère Esther touched my arm. I should begin with those I might be able to save, she said quietly.

Save? I could do nothing here! What could I do for men whose limbs and bodies were so torn and shattered?

"Do what you can, Geneviève," she whispered. "It is all any of us will do this day."

I tended the wounded as well as I could. Now and again M. Laparre would call to me to assist him. I hardened myself to the screams of men whose legs or arms he was amputating, although it was sickening and pitiful. The men I nursed were faceless to me.

All the while there were only two faces for which I watched, and with each passing hour I thanked *le bon Dieu* that I saw neither.

Très tard

I returned to the house and took off my moccasins and the rest of my Abenaki clothing. It is now in my chest. I know that it is only clothing, as are the familiar garments I once again wear, but somehow it is as though I have put a piece of myself away with them. I must not think or write of such foolishness.

Word has spread through the town that Montcalm is wounded. Who will lead the army? How will the town be defended without him?

Le 14 septembre 1759
Quelques heures avant l'aurore

One of the sisters shook me awake this night and gave me a basket, saying that M. Laparre wanted me to go to the house of M. Arnoux, the apothecary, and bring back all the camphor, yarrow and poppy that I could find.

I stepped over sleeping men and walked past dying men, saying a prayer for the safety of Étienne and my brother. The low moans of those in pain rose up in the darkness. Outside, the sky was sparkling with stars and the air was fresh and sweet, just as though nothing at all had happened, just as though Québec was still safe. I entered the apothecary's house and saw that it was filled with French officers. One of them raised a finger to his lips. Someone must be in the bedroom beyond.

Quietly, so as not to cause a disturbance, I found what M. Laparre had asked for and filled the basket. It was then I saw that many of the officers were openly weeping. From the room came voices, one of which was M. Arnoux's.

"You are dying, monsieur. You have only hours."

"So much the better," came the weak reply. "I am happy I shall not live to see the surrender of Québec."

I respectfully asked one of the officers who it was that lay within, that I might say a prayer for him.

"Ah, mademoiselle," he said, his tears running freely. "It is Général Montcalm. He was wounded this morning on the field of battle, and although with help he was able to ride his horse back into the town . . . " He shook his head.

I crept from the house and brought M. Laparre the medicines. I have prayed for Chegual and for Étienne. And for Général Montcalm. There is nothing to do but wait and fight the despair that tries to rise up in my heart.

Le matin

We have been abandoned to the enemy. The army is gone and with it Vaudreuil. *Sacré* cowards!

Général Montcalm has died.

Pendant la nuit

It was done so quickly, with none of the tributes that should have been paid a great officer. A coffin was hastily constructed by one of the Ursulines' old servants, a man called Bonhomme Michel. Général Montcalm's body was placed inside it. It was decided that the safest place for his remains would be right inside the Ursuline monastery, where an exploding shell had created a deep hole in the chapel floor.

At nine o'clock this night the coffin was carried slowly through the street followed by Commandant de Ramezay and a military escort. With the others I went to the chapel and stood with my head bowed as Père Resche said the prayers by torchlight. *Libera me, Dominum.* Then we left the général's coffin alone in the chapel with the soldiers who would cover it with earth.

Now, late this night, I cannot help but think of Montcalm, whose body had to be buried in secret.

What sort of men are these British, if it was necessary to hide Montcalm away? What might they have done to his remains? And what will they do to us if they take the town?

Le 15 septembre 1759

The remaining militia are deserting the town, they say, and many of our Abenaki allies are gone. People are calling for Commandant de Ramezay to surrender. I hope that Chegual and Étienne, they who would never desert, will come soon.

Le 18 septembre 1759

Québec has surrendered to the British. I no longer believe in miracles.

Plus tard

The British army has entered the town. Their flag now flies over us. I have taken knives and hidden one in each of my pockets. If my brother were here, he would defend us, and the helpless wounded for whom we care, as would Étienne.

Where can they be?

Le 19 septembre 1759

When the wind blows off the battlefield where still so many bodies lie, all I can smell is death.

Le 21 septembre 1759

The Ursuline sisters have returned to their monastery at last. Mme Claire and I went with them to be of help. It should have given them great joy. It should have been a time for prayer and thanksgiving, but instead the convent is to be occupied by the British! Their Général Wolfe is dead and an officer called Général James Murray now commands the army. He has ordered all this.

I am ill with worry.

Le 22 septembre 1759

The only happiness I can write of is that a couple — a certain Marie-Louise Pepin and Jean-Pierre Massal — have been wed in the Ursuline chapel.

As for other matters, Mme Claire has made the decision to help the sisters at the monastery hospital that will be set up. I have considered feigning illness, weakness and even madness rather than give help to the enemy. For they *are* my enemies, these *barbares*.

If I do not soon hear word of my brother and Étienne, I fear I *will* go mad.

Le 23 septembre 1759

We are expected to swear loyalty to the British king. If we do so, we will be given soldiers' provisions. I will never do that. I will starve first.

Le 26 septembre 1759

No word. I have no heart to write.

Le 30 septembre 1759

Can we be more betrayed than this? The British soldiers have taken all manner of fine goods from the intendant's storehouse. Hosiery, firearms, clothing, gold and silver laces, clocks — *clocks!* — all these things the *cochon* Bigot was hoarding for himself while the people of this town have done with so little all this time.

No word of Étienne or my brother.

Le 1er octobre 1759

No word.

Le 2 octobre 1759

The British held what they called Divine Service in the Ursuline Chapel today. This they will do on Wednesdays and Sundays from now on, Mère Esther has told us. Some of the merchants, men I scarcely know, were in attendance. *Huguenots!* Have they been practising their Protestant religion here all along?

It is all inconceivable.

Le 5 octobre 1759

What has happened can scarcely be believed. The entire world has turned upside down. The Ursuline monastery is filled with the vile Scots in their *stupide* skirts! The bottom floor will be used as a military hospital for the men. Général Murray will have his headquarters in the parlour and the sisters will be accorded their privacy on the upper floor. How generous of him.

Mère Esther has said that all will be treated with equal kindness, with the same tenderness with which we would treat our own people. All are the same in God's eyes.

Not in my eyes.

Pendant la nuit

I will not nurse the enemy, the Scots animals whose presence defiles the monastery. I will ignore the requests of the British Doctor Russell whom we have been told will be in charge. There. I have written it down and nothing can make me change my mind. None of them will receive a kind touch from me.

I have shut the door upon my conscience today and turned from any task that involves the enemy. That foul work I leave to the others who have the stomach for it. I will do nothing to ease their suffering.

Le 6 octobre 1759

I thank *le bon Dieu* with every fibre of my being. Only now, after fearful hours of work and worry may I write this. Chegual, although badly wounded, is here with me at the monastery hospital at last. Two Abenaki warriors, men who would not normally be in the town, brought him to the monastery. He wanted to come here to die in the presence of his sister, said one of the men as they left.

I screamed for someone to help me, for anyone to help me. One of the surgeons shook his head and said that I should make Chegual as comfortable as I could. With that injury there was little hope.

His skin was grey from loss of blood. He had taken a terrible wound in his thigh, and the muscle was slashed to the bone. But someone, perhaps one of the warriors, had tied a tourniquet around his leg and now the bleeding had diminished to a slow ooze.

I stared at my brother and was filled with such rage that surely everyone in the room must see it blazing in me. I will not lose you! I hissed at him. Then, alone — for clearly they thought it was time wasted — I cleansed the wound and stitched it, and bound it with herbs. He had other wounds, smaller ones, and those I cleansed as well. I wrapped a blanket around him and said a prayer to St. Jude. There was nothing more I could do. All day I stayed at Chegual's side to make certain there was no bleeding or fever, at least not yet.

Étienne is still outside the town walls, but so are many other men, I have been told. That gives me hope.

Tard

I dare not leave Chegual, in spite of both Mère Esther's and Mme Claire's protests. If I were to be asleep at the house and —

No. Nothing will happen to him. Not if I am here.

Le 7 octobre 1759

Chegual is sleeping now. He awoke and spoke to me and was able to take a bit of bread and broth.

He made light of his wound, saying, "It is only a scratch, Geneviève. How can I not heal when it is your hands that have seen to it?" Then he raised himself up on one elbow and stared at the wounded men — the enemy — that surrounded him.

"What of Étienne?" I asked him in Abenaki. "Did you see him?"

"He is well," Chegual assured me, and said that it would take more than a man dressed like a woman to stop Étienne. One of the sisters called to me then, and so I stood, but not before I kissed Chegual's forehead and whispered that he *would* get well and his leg *would* be whole again.

Then I put my hands together, closed my eyes and prayed harder than I have ever prayed in my life that Chegual would heal quickly and that Étienne was safe. When I opened my eyes, I noticed that one of the Scots was watching me. His left hand was wrapped in a filthy, blood-soaked cloth. I turned away from him, fighting the anger that was rising in me. How dare that *sauvage* with hair the colour of a carrot stare while I prayed!

Now I sit on the floor, a blanket over my shoulders, trying to compose myself for what sleep I may be able to get. I have felt Chegual's forehead. It is not overly warm and he is resting peacefully. Again the skirted *sauvage* observed what I did with no care for our privacy. He continues to stare as I write this.

I suppose he knows no better and is to be pitied.

Le 9 octobre 1759

I have examined Chegual's wound and although sadly there is no pus — pus naturally being a sign that the ill humours are draining — the flesh is cool and not swollen. My mind now is filled with worrisome thoughts of Étienne, but I cannot give up hope.

Le 10 octobre 1759

I roll bandages. I clean and cook. I will not touch the scum by whom I am surrounded. Chegual was feverish and so I gave him yarrow tea to help him sweat.

Le 12 octobre 1759

Étienne is dead.

Le 14 octobre 1759

I write of Étienne's death only because he must not be forgotten.

They brought in his body two days ago, saying that he had been wounded in a skirmish only the night before. I wept until were no more tears within me. I hate the British. We buried Étienne in Hôtel-Dieu's cemetery.

At first Mme Claire would not let me see him. She felt that it would be best to remember him as he was. "I must see him one last time," I said, and so I went to the room where our dead lay.

He was so still and white.

I washed his hands and face and combed his hair, trying not to look at the wound that had killed him. Such a small wound, such a small thing to have taken him from us. For a long while I sat with him, thinking of the things we had done and what we would now never do. When men came to take him and the rest of the dead for burial, I can recall thinking that he should have better than a muddy hole in the ground. He should have had his life.

At least there was a casket. Mme Claire had Bonhomme Michel quickly build it out of the big armoire in her bedroom. I laid a pillow and then a soft, clean blanket inside the casket. When they placed him in it, I wrapped the blanket around Étienne, forcing myself to look at his face so that I would never forget this moment. Then we followed as the men carried his casket and other bodies to the cemetery. I did not listen as Père Segard said the prayers over him. I did not watch as they lowered the casket into the ground.

My cross, that I gave him for luck, for the love of *le bon Dieu*, is there with him.

Pendant la nuit

I did not want to tell Chegual of Étienne's death, but I did. My brother said nothing at first, and then I saw pain — a pain greater than what his wound causes him — twist his face. I thought I had no more tears, but I was wrong. I wept again for our loss, for our Étienne. Chegual reached out and took my hand.

"Dry your tears, my sister," he said. "He died a

warrior's death. That is a good thing."

I was sobbing now, and a few of the older sisters who do not give way to such weakness and emotion were casting looks my way. I did not care.

"But I miss him so," I said to Chegual, and he squeezed my hand, holding it until I was able to control myself. I wiped my eyes with my apron and straightened my back. It was then that I saw — yet again! — the rude Scot watching us. I wanted to scream at him, to slap his face, and it was only Chegual holding onto my hand very tightly, knowing my feelings, that stopped me.

I can scarcely believe what happened next. The Scot nodded his head to me, his face serious, and said something. I have no idea what it was or even if he was speaking to me or to himself, for he spoke a horrible language that made no sense at all.

It was probably some foul, cruel remark. I have put it from my mind.

Le 19 octobre 1759

Most of the British ships are gone, having sailed yesterday. I could hear them firing their cannons twenty-one times. Only a few vessels remain, they say, among them the small ships *Porcupine* and *Racehorse*.

How confident the British must be.

Le 21 octobre 1759

Today was the feast of Ste. Ursula and a special Mass was said. There is a statue here of Ste. Ursula with an arrow in her hand. How often I have looked upon that statue. She died a martyr, the arrow being a symbol of her holy death.

I would never compare myself to a saint, and yet with the death of Étienne, I too am pierced with loneliness.

Le 24 octobre 1759

It takes all my will to even write one word today. How I miss him. You were a hero to me, Étienne.

Le 25 octobre 1759

I went to the chapel tonight and stood by the grave of Général Montcalm. "They are here," I whispered. "You died and so did not have to see it, but we will see them every day until we too are gone. Québec is no longer French. It is British."

I am not certain what I expected to happen. Nothing, I suppose.

Étienne.

Le 26 octobre 1759

Word has come of a horrible, sickening thing. Rangers have attacked and burned the St. Francis mission in an act of revenge. They killed our people and took others prisoner, their fate being so hideous that I cannot bring myself to write it. I did not know these Abenaki, these men, women and children, but still I wept.

Chegual's rage was unspeakable.

Avant l'aurore

"What if I had taken you there?" Chegual whispered to me last night in the darkness.

"But you did not," I answered him.

"We could be dead now. The Rangers might have taken you and — "

I put my fingers over his lips. "But it did not happen. It was not our time to die. Now sleep," I told him.

I know the Scot was listening to us as he always does. I could see his eyes glittering. Did it please him that innocent people were made to suffer in such a way?

Le 27 octobre 1759

Today began much the same as the others, with floors to be washed with vinegar and food to be cooked. Then, as I carried an armful of bandages to where M. Laparre was working, I heard him speak.

"It must come off."

He was addressing an officer, one who spoke French, who was standing next to the Scot who stares so. Their Doctor Russell seemed to be in agreement. When M. Laparre picked up his screw tourniquet, the Scot shook his head and said something to the officer. He spoke in their barbaric, incomprehensible language which sounds even worse than English. But the meaning was clear. He was refusing to have his hand amputated.

The officer answered him and again the meaning was clear, for he spoke as one very used to commanding. I set down the bandages and turned away. What did I care for any of this?

"I will need your assistance, Mademoiselle Aubuchon," M. Laparre called to me over his shoulder.

I knew what he wanted. I had done it before at Hôtel-Dieu. Any blood must be mopped as he cut so that he could see what he was doing. I shook my head to make it clear I would not touch the Scot. "I will have nothing to do with the animals who have killed someone I loved and who have destroyed our city."

I was not whispering. The area around us grew silent and the hands of every nun within hearing flew to their mouths.

"Geneviève!" one of the sisters cried out. "What can you be thinking? This is not like you at all." I did not move. I recall now that I was thinking of Étienne, and my brother's terrible wound and the sight of my world in ruins.

Then the wounded Scot spoke. In French! French so oddly accented it was barely understandable. "Mademoiselle need not trouble herself. I will cause her no more suffering than she has already endured." And he turned his face away.

For some reason I looked across the room. Mère Esther and Mme Claire were watching. I met their eyes and saw pity in them . . . and then I slowly realized that the pity was for me. I can still feel the shame that filled me at that moment. I turned and watched as they strapped the Scot to the bed. The officer gave him rum — a great deal of rum — from a flask. It would help deaden the pain. M. Laparre turned to another patient, for it would take a few minutes for the rum to begin to work on the Scot. Still I did not move.

Someone called to me to do something or another. To be truthful, I do not recall what it was. "I cannot," I answered. "I am needed here." I took from my pocket the thick piece of leather I keep there. It was once smooth, but now it is pitted by tooth marks. I told the Scot to bite on it, that it would help.

He turned his face to me, anger and pain making his features harsh. But he did as I bid him. He did not cry out once, not when M. Laparre cut into his flesh, not when the veins and arteries were cauterized, not when the bone saw severed his hand just above the wrist, not when the surgeon drew the flaps of skin over the stump. He worked as quickly as he could, and it took only a few minutes, but I knew well that it had seemed like an eternity for the Scot.

M. Laparre asked me to finish, to sew the skin together with a needle already threaded. Even then the Scot did not make a sound. He simply lay there, his face and lips white. Afterward I removed the tourniquet slowly to make certain there was no bleeding. There was none, for my stitches were perfect. Then I dressed the stump. I took the leather from between the Scot's teeth, turned my back on him and left the infirmary.

Now I am not certain why I helped at all.

Le 28 octobre 1759
Tard ce soir

Chegual was well enough for me to return with Mme Claire to the house this evening to bathe and change my filthy, blood-spattered clothing. I had decided to sleep here for the first time in many days. And dear little Wigwedi! Madeleine had been caring for her all this time. I picked up my rabbit and hugged her, ignoring the risk of her vengeance. La Bave! How she barked in her joy to see me.

Mme Claire came to my room once I was clean and settled in my bed, Wigwedi at my side.

"Ah, Geneviève," she said. "You have grown up this summer, I fear. Quickly. Far too quickly." Then she put her arms around me, saying she had hoped I could have been spared all this.

I protested that my place was and is here.

She took my hands in hers and told me that life is filled with terrible trials that wound us deeply. "I wish that you had not learned this lesson at so young an age," she said, "but we are given no choice in such things."

I had no idea what to say.

"Wounds leave scars, Geneviève. Sometimes those scars cannot be seen," she went on. I think that what she said next moved me as no words ever have. "The very saddest, I think, is a scarred heart. One that can no longer feel." Then she kissed my cheek and told me to get what rest I could.

I do not think I will sleep tonight. I have made a difficult decision. It has eased my heart some, but not much. In the morning I will confess to Père Segard.

I have much to confess.

Le 29 octobre 1759

Père Segard said nothing at first. He simply sat in the darkness of the confessional while I waited in misery for my penance. Then I heard a deep sigh come from beyond the confessional screen. His words are with me yet.

"I think you have been doing penance for many days, my child," he said. "Bitterness and cruelty are not part of your nature. You have suffered and then sought to strike out the only way you could.

That God's goodness works within you, Geneviève, is proved by the fact that, in the end, you did not turn from an enemy when *he* was suffering. But still, it is my duty as your confessor to give you a penance, and so for your penance you will do good works."

He said the words of absolution and they gave me comfort just as they always do. Then he coughed. My penance? Only one good work would be necessary. "You will nurse the Scot until he is well. I will arrange with Mère Esther that you have few other duties. Go in peace, Geneviève."

Peace? I think I will never know peace again.

Le 30 octobre 1759

I returned to the infirmary today. I can recall thinking that my penance would be difficult, but in the end I was wrong.

It was hideous.

The Scot wanted to be in my presence no more than I wanted to be in his. He who stared so often, would not look at me now. He would only let me change his dressing when ordered to do so by his général. He would not eat unless ordered to. He simply lay there, his face turned to the wall.

I finally lost all patience.

"You like me no better than I like you, *sauv* — monsieur," I said, "for we are enemies, but you are my penance."

He turned his angry eyes to me. "Your penance, mademoiselle?"

Of course, he would know nothing of that, being ignorant of my faith. I told him I had confessed my sins as good Catholics do. Hating him and all his kind was one of them. "My penance for this sin is to nurse you until you are well. The sooner you are healed, the sooner you may be rid of me."

He gave me an odd look. "Very well, mademoi selle. Who am I to stand in the way of such a sacred thing. Do your best. Or your worst, if you must."

At the moment I thought little of what he said, but now I can see he was making light of me.

Le 31 octobre 1759

Today one of the other Scots came to me when I was with Chegual. He spoke at length in English and then watched my face.

I asked my brother what the man wanted. I could barely understand his words.

"Nothing," Chegual answered. The man wishes to thank me — all the Scots wish to thank me — for my treatment of the one who lost his hand. "*Une Main*, I am calling him," my brother told me, "although they say his real name is — "

I held up my hand. I have no wish to know his name.

Le 1er novembre 1759

Cook says that there is bad talk of Gouverneur Vaudreuil. *Quelle surprise.* With so many of the men gone, the women are reproaching him, since all the farm work must fall to them. Cook says that one very angry woman cried that he may be brought to as miserable and barbarous an exit as ever a European suffered under savages.

Indeed.

We went to Mass this morning since it was All Saints' Day. I prayed that Étienne is at peace. There is no longer any hope of that for me.

Le 2 novembre 1759

The nuns are using their own linen for bandages. At Mme Claire's direction, we have brought sheets and cloths and old clean *chemises* from the house. I am exhausted each night and go to sleep almost at once.

Le 4 novembre 1759

They are saying that Général Murray has divided Québec into counties. Does he think he is the king here? *Le Roi Murray?* It appears so. And he is taking wine from the king's stores. He has passed out more than sixty hogsheads to his officers.

Yet there was one thing today that amused me. Murray's soldiers could not get up to the Haute-Ville because of the ice. An entire company of them slid down the hill.

Le 6 novembre 1759

The house that Général Montcalm had used as his headquarters is now being called *Candiac* after his birthplace. I try to find pity in my heart for him, he who lies buried so far from home.

Le 8 novembre 1759

Laws, laws, laws, British laws! Lights must be out by ten. If you are out walking at night you must have a lantern and you will be taken prisoner if you do not. Carriages may not stop near any gateway. People say that British justice is no harsher than French. To me it is like slavery.

Le 10 novembre 1759

Québec's streets are now lit by lamps each night, lamps made by the British tinsmiths. At first I thought that with the snow falling it was somehow beautiful. Then I realized that the lamps only let us see the destruction that night hides.

How I miss Étienne.

Le 11 novembre 1759

Just when I am certain I am beginning to come to terms with how our lives have changed, I am filled with confusion.

This morning, before Sunday Mass began, Mme Claire and I sat in prayer. Other people were there of course and the sisters were on the other side of the grille waiting in privacy.

Then I saw him.

It was the Scot, Une Main, entering the chapel. He had a black arm band upon the sleeve of his coat. Why was he here? Would he laugh and mock our faith? Then he took a rosary from his pocket, blessed himself and began to tell his beads. I could not concentrate on the Mass, I could not pray, I could not even think clearly.

Later I spoke to Père Segard. There are Catholics among the Scots, he told me. Général Murray desires that they should not practise their faith openly — why does this not surprise me? — but they are not *forbidden* to attend Mass and receive the sacraments.

The black arm band? Général Murray has asked that all his officers wear it as a sign of their mourning for Général Wolfe.

We are a city of mourners.

Le 13 novembre 1759

Wintry weather today.

Le 15 novembre 1759

Warmly dressed in heavy clothing and my wool cape, I walked to the site of the Abenaki encampment this afternoon in the company of Bonhomme Michel. Since I am known to work at the monastery hospital, the soldiers did not trouble us, although they closely question anyone coming into or leaving the town.

It was such a lonely place. The remains of a few lean-tos, dead cooking fires, the sound of the wind rattling the bare branches of the trees. Then I saw something half buried in the snow, beside a trampled basket. It was a doll, a poor thing made of corn husks and wearing brown woollen cloth.

I picked it up and brushed the snow from it. What girl had loved this doll, held it to her closely, whispered to it in the night? Did she cry sometimes at its loss? Was the girl even alive still?

I might have taken the doll with me. Instead I set it back down and piled snow over it, ignoring Bonhomme Michel's odd look. It seemed better that the doll stay here and, in time, return to the earth instead of being carried back to Québec.

Perhaps the girl's mother, if she lives, will make her another doll after next year's harvest.

Le 17 novembre 1759

A man from our town, one none of us knew, was hanged by the British today for encouraging their soldiers to desert.

Le 19 novembre 1759

I told Chegual about the doll today as I changed his dressing. He was silent for a moment and then he said that I had done the right thing. But after a longer moment he asked me if it was only a doll that I had buried in the snow.

He did not need to say more. I know that I cannot bury the past. Any of it.

Le 21 novembre 1759

Two women were whipped through the streets today for selling rum to the soldiers. Unthinkable.

Le 22 novembre 1759

Any wealthy families who can still afford to do so are leaving for France. The hangings, the beatings, the laws — they are too much.

Le 23 novembre 1759

Frost and snow today. Endless rumours that the French army will march against the town in an attempt to take it back. How I weary of such talk.

Le 25 novembre 1759

The ship *Racehorse* has blown up. Those who survived were brought here with dreadful burns. And Général Murray? It seems what angered him the most was the loss of the ship's carpenters.

Le 26 novembre 1759

I will never become accustomed to the sound and sight of the British army here. March! March!

March! They should march back to England. Chegual laughed when I told him that. I do all I can to cheer my dear brother.

How he mourns Étienne. He says nothing, but his grief is there in his eyes. Can he see mine as well?

Le 28 novembre 1759

I wear two of everything to stay warm. There is a shortage of wood, even though the soldiers are cutting it on Île d'Orleans. They cannot bring it across because of the ice floes in the river and so wood from ruined houses and fences is being used as fuel.

The capitaine of the *Racehorse* has died of his wounds.

Le 1er décembre 1759

Mère Esther says that the soldiers are entirely unprepared for the winter. She is correct, since many suffer from frostbite in this bitter cold. They must go nearly 2 *lieues* to St. Foy to cut wood, eight men pulling a sleigh through the deep snow. How unfortunate for them.

Chegual's leg is healing well. At least there is that blessing.

Le 2 décembre 1759

To relieve the pressure that rests on the shoulders of the sisters, men who do not need constant nursing have been billeted. This will now happen with our household! They have invaded our country. They have taken our town, and now they will occupy our home. I am resigned to nursing them — him — but how can we let a stranger into our home?

Père Segard. If he was not a priest and my confessor, I would — but I had best put that idea out of my head before I find myself with a penance worse than the one with which I am tortured.

Naturally, he heard that more officers are to be billeted, and naturally he is making sure that it is convenient for me to continue with my penance. He spoke with Mère Esther, giving her no details, since it was a matter of a private confession. Mère Esther spoke to Mme Claire and then to Général Murray, who made the necessary arrangements.

Une Main will be billeted in our home, and only he, since he is an officer and such privacy is due his rank.

What of *our* privacy?

Le 3 décembre 1759

Mère Esther took me into the chapel. I thought that she might scold or perhaps ask questions, since she and everyone else surely are curious as to why Père Segard made such a request. I should have known she would not.

He is an officer with the 78th Regiment of Foot commanded by Lieutenant Colonel Simon Fraser, she said, passing on what it appears Général Murray told her. His name is Lieutenant Andrew Guillaume Gordon Doig. When my eyes grew wide at the French name *Guillaume*, she only shrugged. "It is a mystery," she said, "but perhaps in time it shall be solved."

Not by me.

Le 4 décembre 1759

The one good thing that has come of this wretched billeting is that Mme Claire has insisted that Chegual come back to the house immediately. I helped him myself, letting him lean his weight upon me as he limped down the street, a crutch under his arm.

I told him that I would have joyfully carried him on my back, just as he used to carry me when I was small. He laughed aloud at that.

It is the first time he has laughed like that since
— no. I will write of happier things from now on.

Le 6 décembre 1759

It has been necessary to do some shifting about.
Mme Claire will, of course, remain in her chamber. Lieutenant Doig, for all his rank, has refused
to take my room, which is the next best. How gallant of him. It means I must run up and down the
stairs if he requires nursing, but I said nothing.
He is still my penance, after all. He also refused to
take the room off the kitchen that Madeleine and
Cook share. More gallantry.

That left only the drawing room and the library
or maybe the roof, where with luck he would roll
off, but it seemed that the library is to the lieutenant's liking, and so his cot and belongings
were taken there by soldiers. Chegual will sleep in
the kitchen with La Bave, but he will be warm
and dry and safe.

I do not mind running up and down the stairs
for his sake.

Chegual still has a great deal of pain. He says
little, but it shows. Lieutenant Doig's pain is of a
different sort. He says he still feels his hand,
which disturbs him. I will brew up a strong batch

of willow-bark tea for Chegual. And I suppose for the lieutenant.

Doig. What sort of a name is that?

Le 7 décembre 1759

There was a knock on the front door this afternoon. Madeleine was helping Cook with the pastry for *tourtières* and so I answered it. There stood a tall man, a Scot by his uniform, who inquired in French if this was the residence of Lieutenant Andrew Doig.

Non. It was not, Mme Claire answered coolly. She was standing in the hall behind me, a book in her hands. She informed the man that this was her residence and that of her household. "However," she added, "Lieutenant Doig *is* a guest here."

The officer bowed and begged her pardon for the unfortunate misunderstanding. Might he speak with Lieutenant Doig?

I led him to the library. There was a great deal of pummelling of backs and loud greetings in that language with which the Scots somehow manage to communicate. I closed the door and left them to it.

Later, there was a knock on the frame of the

drawing-room door. It was Lieutenant Doig and his companion. He introduced us to the man.

"Madame Pastorel and Mademoiselle Aubuchon, may I present Lieutenant Jonathan Alexander Stewart, also of my regiment. He is my cousin." This man was billeted in the Intendant's Palace, we learned, with many other Scots.

Lieutenant Stewart apologized to Mme Claire for not introducing himself earlier. It was only that he had been unprepared to find a such a lovely lady here. And such a learned one at that, if her splendid library be any indication. He kissed Mme Claire's hand, bowed to me and then saw himself out.

Later I asked her what she made of this fellow. She sniffed and said that she knew little of Scots and nothing at all of Lieutenant Stewart.

"He is literate," she allowed. "He cannot be all bad."

Le 8 décembre 1759

Lieutenant Stewart returned today. He and Lieutenant Doig went for a walk to take the air.

I was able to enjoy the library alone at last. Wigwedi watched me while I searched for a book. She stared, her nose slowly wiggling. Later, I pared vegetables in the kitchen. How her nose wiggled then! I think perhaps her nose wiggling means that she is interested in what is happening around her. I started to think of what Étienne would have made of it, and then stopped myself.

I still cannot believe he is gone from us.

Le 9 décembre 1759

Just now, I crept downstairs for a glass of cider and saw light coming from the library. The lieutenant was writing in what looked to be a journal. He neither heard nor saw me, and so, glass in hand, I went back to my room.

Now I am writing this, and it feels so strange to think that another person is recording his thoughts as well.

Le 10 décembre 1759

It is a thick book with a cover of dark green leather that he leaves on the library table. On the front is inscribed, *Un journal historique des campagnes en Amérique du Nord, pendant les années 1758 et 1759.* I have heard that many of the British officers speak French, but to be writing in French a history of the battles he has experienced? Nothing this man does makes sense.

It sickened me. Within those pages is written the death of my country.

Pendant la nuit

I have read parts of his journal.

Today the lieutenant was escorted by other soldiers to the monastery to meet with his superior, Général Fraser. I decided that the library needed dusting. In particular, the library table. I picked up his journal and gave up all pretenses. I had come here to read it and so I would. Perhaps there would be some useful information within its pages that I could pass on.

Now I wish I had never touched it.

It was written in French, although certain passages were in some other language. It told of battles and skirmishes, of the devastation at Louisbourg and then of sailing up the river to Québec. I read quickly — his hand is neat and clear — for I was uncertain how long he would be away. It was so strange to see the siege through his eyes.

He told of the horrors he had seen this August, of not only what the British and the Rangers had done, but of acts that their enemy, we French and our allies, had committed. No one was innocent of murder and atrocities.

Then I came to September 13, the day of the battle here on the Heights. I read of the wounding of their Général Wolfe. When the général heard that the French were retreating, he said, "Now, God be praised, I will die in peace."

It was hard enough to read of cruelty and war. It was harder to read of how it revolted Lieutenant Doig. One thing written on July 27 remains in my mind.

Général Wolfe has strictly forbidden the inhuman practice of scalping, except when the enemy are indiens *or Canadians dressed as* indiens. *For the love of all that is holy, I can see no difference. They are the enemy, yes, but they are warriors and deserve to be treated as such. I will not permit my men to commit such acts, reminding all of the carnage and cruelty of Culloden. I am an officer, not a butcher.*

I put the book back just as I found it. But still, everything is changed.

Le 11 décembre 1759

As carelessly as I could, I asked Mme Claire about this Culloden.

She thought for a moment and then said, "It was a battle that took place thirteen years past in Scotland. The British crushed the Scots, and they have been subject to them since."

The same thing has just happened to us! We Canadians and Abenakis have lost everything.

Le 12 décembre 1759

My conscience.

I wish I did not have one, but there it is and it pained me dreadfully. I confessed to Père Segard this morning, telling him of my deceitfulness in reading the lieutenant's journal. There was that horrid silence while he considered my sin and what suitable penance he should gave me.

I am not certain I can do this penance.

Plus tard

I thought it best to complete my penance quickly. I went to the library and stood before Lieutenant Doig, my hands behind my back. He asked if he might be of service.

"Yes," I answered, and I brought out my hands, one of which held my journal. "I wish you to read this."

"Your journal, mademoiselle? It is doubtless a very private thing. Why should I violate what privacy you are managing to have, with me here?" he asked.

And so I told him what I had done and how my penance was to let him read my journal in return.

He said he accepted my offer, "so that your penance may be fulfilled," but he refused to read my journal. "And furthermore, you may read mine whenever you wish." He went on to add that he was not the only officer keeping a journal. A certain Lieutenant John Knox had been writing his account of the war as well. Then he said, "But Lieutenant Knox is a British officer, and I suspect his perspective is rather different than mine. I intend to have this journal published some day, so that all may read my account of what has happened here."

I am not certain how I feel about that.

Le 13 décembre 1759

There is something growing between them, between Lieutenant Doig and my brother. The lieutenant is but three years older than Chegual. I had thought him much older, but then he is a soldier and has seen and done many difficult things, I suppose. One would think they had little in common, a Scot and an Abenaki. But they are both warriors, and Chegual's breechcloth is much like a kilt, which is what the lieutenant calls what he wears. The Scots have clans, as do the Abenaki, Chegual has told me. And they have chieftains.

The kilts, though! At least a breechcloth covers a man, while a kilt is simply a skirt. And there is worse. The Scots wear nothing at all beneath them! Since the Scots have no breeches, the Ursulines are calling them *les gens sans culottes*. They are knitting long stockings for them so that they will not, well, so that . . .

I shiver to think of such a thing during a Québec winter.

Mme Claire, who never throws out anything, still has some of her drowned cousin's clothing in an *armoire*. She has insisted that both Chegual and Lieutenant Doig wear these things. How comical Chegual looks in breeches!

Le 14 décembre 1759

Today, soldiers who were going out to cut wood said they would deliver some here. Lieutenant Doig, who would not have been cutting wood under any circumstances, watched them leave and then walked away with a disturbed expression on his face.

I found him in the library, staring out the window. I saw him before he saw me. I walk like a nun, he told me. Silently. Unlike my rabbit, whose claws make a sound against the wood floors. Shall I pound my heels? I recall thinking. I did not say it aloud, though.

I set a cloth-covered bowl on the table. Ointment. I told him that if it is massaged onto his wound twice a day, it might speed the healing.

To myself I thought, And my penance will mercifully be over.

Le 15 décembre 1759

Chegual has confessed to me in private that he likes Lieutenant Doig. He said, "I should hate him. I should call him out to battle, but I have no heart for more killing. Not for the sake of Québec."

Chegual is a warrior. I have accepted that. What will he do with his life if he never goes into battle again?

Le 16 décembre 1759

A day of surprises.

Lieutenant Stewart escorted Mme Claire to Mass this morning. They walked behind the rest of us and Lieutenant Doig walked next to me. He was not escorting me, of course. He had to walk next to someone, I suppose, and it happened to be me.

Then this afternoon! I was startled when I saw Chegual and Lieutenant Doig armed with muskets, knives and tomahawks, until Chegual said that they were going out to hunt. I stared at the lieutenant's arm, at the place where his hand should be. He had pinned the cuff of his sleeve closed.

Chegual left the house but I asked the lieutenant to wait while I ran up to my room. "Here," I told him a moment later. I had made this and several more like it for him, I explained — only as part of my penance, he was to understand — but I did not think he would require them so soon. It was a straight stocking of soft, red wool. It would protect . . . Then, I fear I faltered.

"My stump, mademoiselle? *Merci* for your kindness. Will you please assist me?"

For all my nursing, for all I have seen and done, slipping the stocking over the end of his arm was somehow one of the hardest. "Will it do?" I asked.

"Aye," he said. "It will do well, mademoiselle. It will do well."

Lieutenant Doig came back exhausted, as did Chegual, but I believe both of them were content. Between them he and Chegual had devised a method so that the lieutenant may fire his weapon. Neither of them shot a single thing. Still, I believe the hunt was successful.

What can *aye* possibly mean?

Le 17 décembre 1759

Lieutenant Stewart arrived on our doorstep yet again today. When Madeleine told him that Lieutenant Doig was not here, he did not seem the least bit disappointed.

"I am calling on Mme Pastorel," he said. "If she is at home and receiving visitors."

Madame was at home, and she received Lieutenant Stewart and called for a pot of hot chocolate. Then they went into the library. Madeleine and Cook could not stop giggling. In time, Lieutenant Stewart left, a book in his hand.

I asked what he had borrowed.

François de La Rochefoucauld's *Maximes*, Mme Claire told me. Lieutenant Stewart said his favourite of the sayings is number 119: *We are so used to disguising ourselves from others that we end by disguising ourselves from ourselves.*

Now that I think on it, that sounds like me.

Le 18 décembre 1759

Wigwedi is able to jump amazingly. I have calculated that could I jump as high as she, I would be able to leap onto the roof of the house. Today she leapt onto the table in the library. I offered to remove her, since Lieutenant Doig was seated there reading, but he waved aside my offer.

"She is an interesting creature," he said thoughtfully. "One would almost think she had a mind of her own."

"Of course she has a mind," I countered. "It is a rabbit mind, but a mind nonetheless."

He laughed. I have never heard him laugh before.

Le 19 décembre 1759

Général Murray is generous. He is not a man I can easily like, but it is the truth. He is stiff and impatient and cannot seem to understand ordinary people. Still, he has made certain that the monastery has been kept supplied with not only wood, but with food. Because our household shelters an officer, some of those courtesies are extended to us.

This afternoon the cook from the *Porcupine* is coming to our house to prepare a meal for Lieutenant Doig and so, of course, for us. At Mme Claire's invitation, Lieutenant Stewart will attend. I can remember the wonderful food we had aboard Capitaine Guyot's ship so many months ago. It is said that British cookery is very different from ours, but it seems they have slaughtered a pig, something that any good cook may be able to prepare nicely.

What a feast we shall have.

Le 20 décembre 1759

Potatoes were brought into this kitchen, much to our horror! Cook nearly fainted. Potatoes are nothing but animal food, as everyone knows.

"A civilized person will not eat them, even when starving," I told Lieutenant Doig as we sat at the table awaiting the meal. I could feel the old prejudices rising up inside me. Really! I thought. Surely they cannot actually expect us to eat potatoes.

He was silent a moment and then his face darkened. I cannot forget his angry words. He said, "But you have not experienced starvation, have you, mademoiselle? Hunger perhaps, but not a hunger so great that you will eat anything, no matter how repulsive. To one facing true starvation, potatoes would be a luxury."

The entire table grew silent.

Lieutenant Stewart cleared his throat and said that I had not truly dined until I had dined upon Royal Navy victuals. He assure me that there was nothing like it in the world.

Then the cook brought in the food. "Lobscouse and soused pig face," he said proudly. There lay the face surrounded by greasy potatoes and unidentifiable things.

"Where is the rest of the pig?" Mme muttered.

After the meal, the cook announced a dessert was coming. A *compote* of fruit and *eau de vie*, perhaps? But, no. It was something all quivering called a *spotted dog*. Mme Claire is too well-bred to have said a word, but her face said all.

Lieutenant Stewart laughed aloud. "It is only a boiled suet pudding with currents and prunes, madame and mademoiselle. Not a shred of dog went into it."

I may never be the same. The grease has set my bowels to . . . well, I am not myself.

I suppose in some ways the dinner was a success, but Lieutenant Doig's sour mood was not. He barely said a word all evening.

Le 21 décembre 1759

Where to begin here? With our apologies to each other for our remarks, Lieutenant Doig and I?

No. I will begin with starvation. And with Culloden.

Lieutenant Doig's father fought against the British in that battle in 1746. The British put down the Scots' uprising and their attempt to bring back their own king to Scotland. Lieutenant Doig was but a child of six years. He nearly starved that winter after his father died in battle. Many did, for the British had burned their crops. In the end his mother did die — from giving her food to him, he is certain. In the spring he was taken to France where his grandparents lived. Thus the name *Guillaume*, which is his *grand-père*'s.

When Lieutenant Colonel Fraser, Lieutenant Doig's commander, formed his Highland Regiment two years ago, Lieutenant Doig bought his commission and joined. As a soldier in this regiment, he would again be able to wear a kilt. Since Culloden, no Scot may wear the garment under pain of death, nor may their clans gather any more. It gives the lieutenant great joy to wear his kilt. He has no love for the British crown, any more than Chegual has for the French. They are both but a means to an end, he told me, to redeem the honour of Scotland and his people.

"In spite of the cost?" I asked him. "How can we forget all that? All the people we loved who are gone now?"

"One takes strength in memories," he said.

I will eat potatoes uncomplainingly from now on.

Le 22 décembre 1759

Wigwedi has taken to begging. This she has often done with me, but it is Lieutenant Doig upon whom she now fixes her attention. Cats will jump onto the lap of a person who dislikes them. The lieutenant does not dislike rabbits, but he is an unlikely candidate for rabbit affections. Still, there you are.

Today she stared at him. Then she nudged his leg. I thought it would go no further, but she raised herself up and stood with her front paw on his calf. "What does it want?" he asked me, clearly amused.

She, I told him. I explained that she wanted his apple, that she was begging.

He laughed and said that he supposed that he must give her a bit of it, so he did not insult her. Then he looked at me sideways. "For that would be a grave error in rabbit etiquette," he said. "A serious *faux paw.*" He smiled and asked if I had caught the joke.

"What joke?" I asked.

He confessed that Mme Claire had told him that I speak some English.

"Only a little," I admitted. What else had she told him? I thought.

"In English, a rabbit's foot is a *paw,* a word that sounds much like *pas,* and is spelled *p-a-w.* A *faux paw,* a mistake in rabbit etiquette?"

It took me a moment to grasp the joke.

The lieutenant looked down at Wigwedi as he fed her a bite of apple. Then he said, "She does very well with only three legs."

Indeed, I answered, and I told him about Wigwedi and the lynx. An ordinary rabbit might not have been able to survive such a thing, but she is no ordinary rabbit, I said. She had not let the loss of a mere leg . . . I stopped then, and put both hands over my mouth, for I realized with horror what I was saying and how I would be hurting his pride.

"I have already taken a lesson from your brave little rabbit, mademoiselle," he said. "I cannot let myself be bested by a rabbit, can I? Even one that is no ordinary creature."

No. I answered, still very embarrassed. That *would* be a grave *faux paw.*

How he laughed at that.

Le 23 décembre 1759

Potatoes are one thing, but now it is tea. I have only had the drink when I am ill, and then it is brewed as strongly as possible, so that the most good may be got from it. It is a medicinal drink, after all.

The day was brisk. When Lieutenant Doig and Lieutenant Stewart returned from a long walk, they asked for tea. Perhaps they are feeling un-well, I thought, and so I brewed a good, strong pot. I poured for them. They were speaking with Mme Claire and so they simply nodded their thanks. Lieutenant Doig took a sip without look-ing into his cup and immediately began to choke. What was this? he gasped.

Lieutenant Stewart was coughing, crying out that he was poisoned!

I assured them that it was tea, black and strong as it should be. How could it do them any good otherwise?

Any *wee lassie* could make tea properly, I was told. Lieutenant Doig exclaimed that he could stand his sword up in it! And then I suppose he saw the expression on my face. "Which is precisely the way we like it. *Oui,* Jonathan?" He sipped again, his eyes watering. I stood there and watched them drink the entire pot.

From now on, even if he is near death, he will make his own tea, if he cannot find himself a *wee lassie* — whatever that is — to do it.

Plus tard

A *wee lassie* is a small girl. *Aye* means yes. His language is Gaelic, which he has spelled for me.

Le 24 décembre 1759

I do not believe in ghosts, yet last night I dreamed of Étienne and he seemed so alive. It was just a dream, of course, for he is gone. And besides, he was in my chamber, sitting on the edge of my bed, holding my hand. And me in a nightdress! Even Étienne with all his forward ways would never have done such a thing in life.

"How are you?" I asked him, and he said that he did well, very well, that there was only one tiny thing keeping peace from enfolding him.

"And what might that be?" I asked.

"Knowing that you are not at peace, Geneviève. Let all of this go and look to tomorrow, not to yesterday. Not with bitterness. Will you promise me that, my dear friend?"

"Yes," I promised.

"Good," he answered. "Be happy, Geneviève." Then he said so very gently, "And watch carefully for friendship, so that you do not miss it when it is offered. That would be a great shame."

I awoke then, the sides of my cheeks wet with tears. Not tears of sadness, but tears of relief, and so I arose from my bed to write this by moonlight. It was just a dream, but somehow I know that Étienne is at peace.

We will attend midnight Mass in a few hours. I will pray for the souls of all who have died in this terrible siege. But most of all I will give thanks that we are alive.

Le 25 décembre 1759

Christmas. It passed quietly today — we exchanged no gifts, only good wishes — and it might have been cheerless but for one thing.

After dinner, Wigwedi was amusing herself by dashing back and forth across the library. In came

La Bave, drooling freely. Then Wigwedi leapt over a chamber pot, spilling the contents everywhere! Now there was more than drool on the floor but, mercifully, liquid only. Soiled linen was folded in a pile near the door. It would be washed tomorrow and so I picked up a sheet with which to mop the mess.

The lieutenant spoke. "Let me do that, mademoiselle. It is my chamber pot, after all. Today of all days there should be no work at all for you on my account."

I stared openly at him and I saw his eyes begin to grow cold. No, I told myself. You promised, and you will not turn aside this gesture.

"Is my penance over, then?" I asked him.

He supposed it was, he answered, looking down at his stocking-covered stump, since Doctor Russell was permitting him to return to full duties in a few days. His next words moved me so. "Perhaps we two could begin again. I offer you my friendship, mademoiselle, if you will accept it."

I accepted, and offered my friendship as well if he wanted it. He did.

Then for no reason at all, I asked him what he had said in his own language the night I told Chegual of the death of our friend Étienne.

Cuimhnich air na daoine o'n d'thainig thuí, he

told me. Knowing I could not understand, he wrote the words on a scrap of paper and gave it to me. Beneath them he had written their meaning in French. *Remember the people from whom you came.*

I will never forget his next words. "We must not forget them. We must remember those who have gone on before us. We are proud of what we are, you and I, mademoiselle — Scot, Abenaki, French and Canadian. We have lost much, but it cannot touch what we are."

Thinking back, I believe I have been given a gift after all.

Le 26 décembre 1759

"Geneviève."

We are Andrew and Geneviève now.

"Your rabbit is on my pillow," he said to me this morning when I brought fresh linen into the library. He picked Wigwedi up and put her on the floor, something I know she dislikes. Then he settled himself into a chair so that he could write.

Then he grumbled, "That animal is yet again on my pillow."

I reached for her, but it was too late. I assured him I would air his pillow and put a clean cover on it. I lifted my shoulders with a helpless sigh. "The rabbit is a vengeful creature, Andrew."

I thought that perhaps the yellow wetness would anger him. I doubt that rabbit urine is something to which he is much accustomed. He only laughed though, and said that he would have to work much harder at winning the affections of one so resistant. Later, when I told my brother what had happened, Chegual asked which of us Andrew had been speaking of, me or Wigwedi? Chegual is becoming as bold as Étienne used to be.

Who indeed?

Le 27 décembre 1759

Andrew is restless and eager to return to his duties. Exercise helps relieve restlessness, so we walked to the monastery hospital today. Mme Claire and I could be of assistance, and Andrew would visit some of his wounded comrades.

How good it was to see Mère Esther and the other sisters. While Mme Claire worked alongside them, I was called to the bed of a wounded Scot. He had miraculously received a letter from his wife Louise, a woman who is French. Alas, he could speak French but not read it. Would I read it to him?

Hoping it contained nothing of a personal nature, I did so. There was news of the farm and the pigs and their cow. Then I read aloud that Louise, *enceinte* when he left home, had given birth.

"To what?" cried the man. His face had grown as pale as milk.

"To a baby," I answered.

"What sort? I beg you tell me!" He grew paler than ever.

I read the rest of the letter and found it. "To a little girl," I told him.

"Another?" he cried. "That makes thirteen! Thirteen daughters."

Men were laughing and calling out teasing remarks about dowries and endless weddings. Then Bonhomme Michel, who was carrying a stack of plates, observed, *"Monsieur, tu es pâle comme un pet de loup!"* Some men were now laughing so hard that they were weeping.

"What does it mean?" Andrew asked me. "How could anyone be as pale as a wolf . . . " He cleared his throat, but could not bring himself to finish, which set the men to laughing harder than ever.

"As pale as a wolf fart?" I said helpfully. I expained that *un pet du loup* is a white mushroom that grows here. A puffball. When you touch them they . . . Now I could not finish because I had begun to laugh.

It felt so good.

Tonight when I prayed I whispered to Étienne that he would have been proud of my boldness. Not even he could have done better.

Le 28 décembre 1759

Andrew has asked if he might cook for us. An officer *cook?* I must have looked surprised.

"I am a Scot first, Geneviève," he answered, "and all Scots can cook."

I was not banned from the kitchen, and so in an hour slipped in. A chicken was simmering in a pot and the smells of garlic and onions met my nose. There should be leeks and prunes instead, he said, pouring in a splash of wine as Cook watched. But there were none. Instead, Andrew would use potatoes.

There were the potatoes on the table, looking like brown lumps of . . . well, like brown lumps. I peeled them the way he showed me, smiling as he teased me for my bravery.

The chicken *ragoût,* something Andrew called *cock-a-leekie,* was delicious. So were the potatoes, I must admit. Even Cook said she had not tasted such fine food prepared by the hands of a man.

Cook was spared the lobscouse and the pig's face, as I recall.

The household has changed so much.

At one time I would not have been working in the kitchen with Andrew at my side. Mme Claire, Madeleine and Cook would not be seated at the kitchen table with my brother lounging in the doorway.

Mère Esther says change can be good. I have come to think she is correct.

Le 30 décembre 1759

Andrew has told us that, in Scotland, something called *Hogmanay* will be celebrated tomorrow night to mark the last day of the old year. Children will go door to door asking for oaten cakes. I told him of our own custom of *Guignolée*.

"*Gui*," he said. "That is mistletoe."

There is no mistletoe here, thank goodness.

Le 31 décembre 1759

Although no one could be out late because of the curfew, still, a good many people came to pay a visit and share a glass of cider. Many of them greeted us by singing "*La Guignolée.*"

Bonjour, le maître et la maîtresse
Et tous les gens de la maison
Nous avons fait une promesse
C'est de venir vous voir une fois l'an
Une fois l'an ce n'est pas grand chose
C'est pour les pauvres.

Some soldiers from Andrew's regiment also arrived. They had with them a curious object. It was a set of *bagpipes,* they said, a musical instrument of Scotland. When one of the men played it, I thought that I had never heard such a sound in all my life, so wild and stirring. And the dance — something Andrew called a highland fling — that the men performed was so spirited. Wigwedi, though, crouched in a corner of her cage, and La Bave ran to the kitchen and hid under the table. They have no appreciation for music, it appears.

Andrew said that it was as enjoyable as Hogmanay.

1760

le 1er janvier 1760

Tard ce soir

How to begin?

This first day of the new year was *aigre-doux*, a mixture of bitter and sweet, for in spite of my best intentions, my thoughts returned often to what has been lost. All the talk this morning after Mass dealt with war, with how the British will attack Montréal, with how the French army will try to retake Québec. I wanted to put my hands over my ears and run screaming through the streets, for I have no more wish at all to talk or even think of war.

Back at the house, Cook's and Madeleine's good food was tasteless in my mouth, Wigwedi's playfulness — she persists in standing on La Bave — and the way La Bave ignores her, held little amusement. The lively conversation of Chegual and Andrew, Lieutenant Stewart's flirting remarks directed to and returned by Mme Claire. Somehow it all did not really touch me.

Then there was a knock on our door. It was M. Leblanc with a crowd of our neighbours. He asked permission to enter the garden behind the house so that they might view the miracle.

"What miracle?" Mme Claire asked him.

"Your hawthorn, madame. They say that in spite of this bitter cold, it is putting forth leaves."

It was. Tiny green leaves had sprouted from the branches. People were whispering that it was a sign that Québec would shake off her oppressors, that she was not conquered after all.

For me it signified something else.

Jigenaz and L'Aubépine? Étienne's Abenaki and French names? They both mean hawthorn. There was a time when I once believed in miracles, and a time this summer when I lost all faith in them. Possibly it is only an accident of nature, for the tree is in a sheltered, sunny spot after all, but perhaps it is finally time to begin believing in miracles once more.

Mère Esther has said that sometimes the most difficult promises to keep are the ones we make to ourselves. They are hard won battles indeed. Well, I vow I will not look back. The war in Canada is not over yet and no one knows what will happen, but I, Miguen, Geneviève Aubuchon, have fought my last battle with the past today.

Epilogue

It would be a lie to say that Geneviève was able to maintain her peace of mind without a struggle, but she was a resilient and determined girl. Her deepening friendship with Andrew, and the love of Chegual and Mme Claire and the rest of the household, were a blessing. Work also helped through the rest of that long and bitter winter. When Andrew returned to his duties, she once again began to volunteer at the school, something that gave her great pleasure. She was also a frequent visitor to the Ursuline hospital, where she cared for anyone who needed her help, regardless of his nationality.

Montréal fell to the British in September of 1760 and Fort Détroit surrendered the next year. When news reached Québec that the Treaty of Paris had been signed on February 10, 1763, making Canada a British possession, the news saddened Geneviève, but it did not crush her spirit.

Andrew's regiment was disbanded that year. Jonathan Alexander Stewart and Mme Claire Pastorel were married, which was no surprise to Geneviève, since the gentleman had been courting Mme Claire with great determination. He was only one of many Scots who remained in Québec.

Unlike Andrew Doig.

When word reached him of his grandfather's death, Andrew sailed for France on September 1, 1763. But not before he had asked Chegual for Geneviève's hand in marriage. Chegual, being a wise young man, agreed. It would mean that Geneviève would have to wait for Andrew for several years until his business in Paris was complete. Geneviève, always very good at keeping promises to those she loved, did just that. Her letters followed him across the Atlantic; his came from Paris and were a great comfort to her during his absence.

Mme Claire, Cook and Madeleine planned a splendid wedding for Geneviève and Andrew during the months before his return. Three days after his ship arrived at Québec on June 7, 1765, he and Geneviève were married in the Ursuline chapel. Mère Esther, who had been elected Mother Superior of the Ursulines some years before, was overjoyed for her former pupil. Although soused pig's face and lobscouse were absent from the wedding feast menu, there were potatoes. And spotted dog.

Andrew had inherited his grandfather's estate and was now a wealthy man. He used some of his inheritance to build a large stone house in the

Basse-Ville on the site of the ruins of Genevieve's girlhood home, property Mme Claire had given to her foster daughter as part of Geneviève's dowry. Andrew purchased land up the street and had a second building constructed where he established a publishing business, Doig & Stewart, in partnership with Jonathan. Andrew's work, *Un journal historique des campagnes en Amérique du Nord, pendant les années 1758 et 1759*, was the first book they printed. The second book published was an account of Culloden.

Chegual, who never married, remained close to Geneviève and her family. Restless and often unsettled, he found that working as a voyageur for a local merchant suited him best. When at Québec, he and Andrew now and again went out to hunt together, both enjoying the wilderness that lay beyond the town. But Chegual did not once return to the site of the ruined St. Francis mission.

Wigwedi and La Bave lived contented, pampered lives. La Bave never again pulled a cart for anyone else but Geneviève and her family. Wigwedi always had the run of the Geneviève's household and remained a vengeful though patient creature to the end of her days.

Geneviève's and Andrew's first child, a boy

they named Étienne, was born in 1767. Within nine years there were five sons. Each of the additional four, David, Guillaume, Seamus and John, were given the middle name of Étienne.

The year 1776 was a difficult one for the family. Late in 1775 Québec again fell under siege; this time it was the forces of the American Revolutionary Army who sought to take the town from the British. Like the other male citizens of Québec, Andrew and Jonathan defended their home all that winter alongside the British soldiers garrisoned there.

The hawthorn tree behind Mme Claire's house died in 1785, the winter that Geneviève gave birth to their sixth child. The baby was a sweet girl whom they named Jeanette, after Andrew's mother. Chegual made a cradle of hawthorn wood for his niece and it was he who gave the baby her Abenaki name *Mategwas*, which means rabbit.

Genevieve's life had its trials. One by one, after long and happy lives, Cook, Mme Claire, Mère Esther and Jonathan all passed away. It was her unfailing love for Andrew and his for her, as well as a certain promise she had made, that kept her from despairing at these losses.

In 1807 Andrew left the family business in the hands of his eldest son. Against all advice — they were elderly, after all — he and Geneviève set sail on a journey that spring. Letters arrived at Doig & Stewart during the next year. Dated April 2, 1808, this was the last.

Dear ones,

So very cold and snowy today, far damper than any Québec winter we have ever experienced. Papa and I have streaming colds that are really little more than annoyances. We are both an amusing sight with our red noses. They keep us indoors. The cold and snow, not the noses.

We are looking forward to boarding our ship in several weeks and returning home. It has been a great joy for Papa to return to visit Scotland. There have been moments quite aigre-doux, *as you can imagine. A last-minute decision to visit the graves of his mother and father today was such a one. Pray for our safe journey.*

All my love,
Maman

It was followed three months later by this letter.

My dear relations,

It saddens me greatly to inform you of the deaths of your parents, who were both taken by pneumonia on April 14 of this year of Our Lord. Knowing their

*time had come, they requested that I make
arrangements that they be buried here on the
hillside. They were certain you would be able to
accept this. Take comfort in the fact that they did
not suffer, and in fact, passed on within hours of
each other.*

*They were remarkable people whose entire lives
were a great adventure. Their stories of the siege of
Québec, of the bravery of the Scots, the Canadians,
the Abenaki and even the British and Americans,
left me speechless. To have made their acquaintance
was my great privilege and honour.*

*Shortly before she peacefully left this life, your
mother asked me to pass on a message. She was
quite insistent that I use her exact words, and so
I have set them here.*

Cuimhnich air na daoine o'n d'thainig thuí.

She said that you would understand.
Your obedient servant,
Willie Doig,
Culloden, Scotland

They understood. The family arranged to have
two bronze plaques cast; on them are their parents' names and Geneviève's message. One of the
plaques was set into a simple stone that marks
Geneviève's and Andrew's resting place on the
hill overlooking Culloden.

Historical Note

On May 28, 1754, twenty-two-year-old Major George Washington and his men attacked a party of French soldiers from Fort Duquesne, at what is now called Jumonville Glen in Pennsylvania. One of the officers, Ensign Joseph Coulon de Villiers, Sieur de Jumonville, was killed. Washington took twenty-one prisoners back to his nearby encampment at The Great Meadow, a large open field. But one Canadian militiaman had escaped. He reported back to Captain Contrecoeur, the fort's commander. Knowing there would be a reprisal, Washington had his men build a small stockade about 16 metres in diameter, one that he called Fort Necessity.

On a rainy July 3, 1754, after a four-hour battle, Washington surrendered the fort to Captain Loius Coulon de Villiers, half-brother of the dead Jumonville. The French and Indian War for the control of North America had begun. Sometimes referred to as The War for Empire, The Seven Years War would not only be fought on this continent, but in Europe, the Caribbean and India. At first the war consisted of skirmishes, but then escalated. For the next few years the outcome would swing back and forth as each side won its victories and forts changed hands.

George II (until October of 1760) and then George III were the kings of England during this period, but the real force behind the war was the prime minister, William Pitt. It was he who ordered that thousands of troops be sent to North America to bring the war to a rapid close by striking at the very heart of New France.

Many of the characters who walk the pages of this story did experience the siege of Quebec. I have attempted to present a balanced picture of what happened during those months. Citizens would not have had instant access to information. Nor would it necessarily be accurate. Geneviève's diary is sometimes coloured by rumours, gossip and time delays, all of which are intentional.

The French and the British had different First Nations allies, although during the siege that summer, it was only the French who were supported by theirs. According to a letter written by Governor Vaudreuil, the allies fighting with the French army and the militia were mainly "Abenakis and different nations of the *Pays d'en Haut*" or upper country. They were skilled warriors who, that summer at Quebec, saw an entirely different sort of warfare, one that was modern. Warriors would have been part of endless raiding parties as they relentlessly harassed the British.

Any man or young man in the city of Quebec would have had to belong to the militia. It was to allow both Chegual and Étienne freedom to come and go that I had Étienne adopted by the Abenaki people. The First Nations allies chose their fights, and sometimes did not fight at all, which showed their good judgment rather than cowardice.

Other than Andrew Doig, James Stewart and young Marc and Louis, all the British and French officers named in the diary were there. It may seem odd that Geneviève is keeping a daily journal under such extreme circumstances, but officers such as Lieutenant John Knox were doing exactly that. So were the captains of the Royal Navy ships, since daily and sometimes hourly log entries were made, which allowed me to pinpoint weather conditions. The hail with which Geneviève and her household chill cider? There was a heavy fall of hail on that very day.

François Bigot, the Intendant of New France, and Pierre de Rigaud de Cavagnial de Vaudreuil, Marquis de Vaudreuil, the Governor, shared the responsibility for running the colony. Bigot was as corrupt as he has been portrayed — not unusual for a colonial officer of the time, at least by modern standards. Vaudreuil, a Canadian, had never commanded a large army and was not pleased to have been replaced by the French general, Montcalm. At times there was disagreement between them, a situation which did not contribute to the French cause. Vaudreuil was convinced that Canada would be able to survive the powerful British offensive that year. Montcalm was less optimistic.

The officer that Geneviève sees on Île d'Orleans is Major General James Wolfe, who had been given the task — his first independent command — of directing a naval attack on Quebec. He was only thirty-two years old, but had been in the military since the age of fourteen. Ironically, Wolfe had been a commander at the battle of Culloden.

He was in poor health that summer, and in fact seemed convinced that he was going to die. Like Montcalm, Wolfe's relationship with his generals — Monckton, his second in command, Murray and Townshend — was not always a co-operative one.

Montcalm's forces consisted of the militia, the regulars from France, and *Les Compagnies Franches de la Marine* (The Independant Companies of the

Navy) — a complement of about 20,000 men. Wolfe had a smaller army, about 9000 men, made up of three brigades of soldiers, as well as the Louisbourg Grenadiers, Light Infantry, Rangers and the Royal Artillery. He could not have taken Quebec had it not been for the Royal Navy and Vice Admiral Charles Saunders and his fleet of 49 warships and 140 other naval vessels, with about 20,000 officers, sailors and *Marines* on board. Not only did the navy bring Wolfe's army safely to the city, it supported it in the summer-long siege. It is interesting to note that Captain James Cook, who would later go on to explore the Pacific and "discover" the Sandwich Islands (now known as Hawaii), was the master or pilot.

An eighteenth-century war, with all its horror and violence, was different in some ways from modern warfare. Geneviève comments upon the flags of truce and the courtliness of the officers. This is no exaggeration. In a letter that Wolfe wrote to General Amherst he remarked regarding the French that " . . . we must teach these Scoundrels to make war in a more gentleman like manner." Perhaps Wolfe did not achieve his goal, but his success at Quebec is undeniable.

Around four o'clock in the morning on September 13, the British ships anchored off Quebec began to bombard the city to create a diversion. At the same time, longboats filled with British soldiers were carried by the tide to L'Anse au Foulon, west of the town. Wolfe's men scaled the cliff and by six o'clock in the morning were in position on what we now call the Plains of Abraham. Sailors had also dragged up two 6-pounders, cannons that fired balls weighing 6 pounds.

At about ten o'clock, the French — militiamen among the soldiers — advanced at a run and their formation began to fall apart. They fired a volley at the British. Wolfe had given orders that no one was to fire until the enemy was about 36 metres away. It was then that the 6-pounders, loaded with grapeshot (a number of small balls), were fired, and the French became disordered. Only when they were closer still did Wolfe give the order to fire what Knox describes as a "well-timed, regular and heavy discharge of our small arms."

The small arms he mentions were muskets loaded with two balls, and the effect was devastating. Black powder creates a great deal of white smoke; it took six or seven minutes for it to clear, but when it did, the British saw that the French were retreating. Fraser's Highlanders gave chase with their broadswords, and the soldiers attacked with bayonets. Hundreds of Canadians — men like Étienne — held them off as the French army fled.

The main battle was over in less than fifteen minutes. Montcalm's army had not stood much of a chance against that of the British. According to Lieutenant John Knox, (though other sources give other figures) 58 British were killed that day and 658 wounded. More Fraser's Highlanders — 168 — were wounded than in any other regiment. Although Vaudreuil says that 44 officers and 600 men were wounded, British accounts claim as many as 1500.

Over the next months many more would die of their wounds. As the story describes, both Wolfe and Montcalm died of their wounds. James Wolfe's body was embalmed and returned to England. He was buried in the family vault at St. Alfege Church in Greenwich. The shell hole in which Montcalm was buried was in time reopened. For many years his skull was on display in the convent. In 2002, however, his remains were moved to the Hôtel-Dieu cemetery where the French soldiers who died during the siege are buried.

Mme Claire's friendship and eventual marriage to Lieutenant Stewart may seem odd, but the fact is that within a few days of Quebec's surrender, Canadian women and British soldiers were marrying. General Murray issued an order forbidding any more of his soldiers from doing this. It would have been necessary for Mme Claire and the lieutenant to wait until the Highland Regiment had been disbanded and he was no longer in the military.

People who had been injured were fortunate to survive wounds in the eighteenth century, since physicians still believed that four internal liquids, called humours — black bile, yellow bile, blood and phlegm — controlled the health and sanity of an individual. When the humours were in balance, all was well. But illness was seen as an imbalance in the humours. There was no concept of infection. The "laudable pus" that Geneviève wished she had seen oozing from Chegual's wound would have been a sign to her that he was getting better. Similarly, the procedure of bleeding a patient, as M. Laparre did with Mme Joule, was another attempt to balance the humours. Regarding the man Geneviève sees buried up to his neck in sand, Lieutenant Knox wrote that it was a cure for scurvy.

The Ursuline monastery was occupied by General Murray and his men for about eight months.

The relationship between Murray and the nuns was a good one. Mère Esther Wheelwright, who had been the assistant superior, was elected superior on December 15, 1760.

Fighting of a different sort continued after the battle. The Rangers, who were not militia, but rather units raised under the British Crown, were ordered by General Amherst to attack the St. Francis mission as an act of revenge once Quebec surrendered. Robert Rogers, the Rangers' leader, claimed that more than two hundred Abenaki were killed; Abenaki accounts say far less. What is known is that several children and a woman who was probably the chief's sister were taken prisoner. This unfortunate woman was killed and eaten by the Rangers when their supplies ran out. Thus Chegual's rage and Geneviève's horror.

It has not been my intention to portray the Rangers or any of King George's forces in a negative light. As Lieutenant Doig's journal shows here, atrocities *were* committed by both sides. Geneviève's reactions to all and any information regarding such events would have been as I have portrayed them: coloured by fear and prejudice.

The Abenaki people took shelter near Quebec after the attack and in time came to live in parts of Quebec, Vermont, Maine and New Hampshire.

Today's United States government still does not recognize the Abenaki as a "tribe," and so the fight for tribal recognition continues.

Quebec has been chosen as a world heritage site by the World Heritage Committee of the United Nations Educational, Scientific and Cultural Organization (UNESCO). Many of the places mentioned in Geneviève's diary may be seen and visited today. Notre-Dame-des-Victoires and the Cathedral have been rebuilt. The Ursuline monastery houses a museum and a collection of artifacts.

War is not simply a list of places and dates. It is more than battles and treaties. War is about people and what it does to them. The siege of Quebec was the longest campaign of the French and Indian War; it changed life forever for the various groups of people who fought with and against each other. But like Geneviève, the people of New France have remained determined and resilient. Their stories and culture remain Canadian treasures today.

French and Indian War Chronology

July 3, 1754 Major George Washington is defeated by the French at Fort Necessity in Pennsylvania.

June 16, 1755 British victory at Fort Beauséjour in Acadia.

July 9, 1755 French defeat of General Braddock's forces near Fort Duquesne. Braddock dies.

September 8, 1755 The British colonial general William Johnson wins the Battle of Lake George.

October 1755 Expulsion of the Acadians begins.

March 11, 1756 Montcalm appointed commander-in-chief of the French forces in North America.

May 18, 1756 Great Britain declares war on France. France declares war on Britain the next day.

August 14–15, 1756 Montcalm takes Fort Oswego.

August 9, 1757 Montcalm takes Fort William Henry.

July 8, 1758 The British fail to take Fort Carillon.

July 27, 1758 General Amherst defeats the French and takes Fortress Louisbourg.

August 27, 1758 The British take Fort Frontenac.

November 25, 1758 The British occupy the site of Fort Duquesne.

June 1759 Siege of Quebec begins.

July 25, 1759 Fort Niagara taken by the British.

July 26, 1759 Fort Carillon taken by the British, who rename it Fort Ticonderoga.

September 18, 1759 Quebec surrenders to the British.

September 8, 1760 Montreal surrenders to the British.

November 29, 1760 Fort Detroit surrenders to the British.

February 10, 1763 The Treaty of Paris is signed. Canada becomes a British colony.

The Catholic nuns in Quebec often took First Nations girls under their wing. Mère Esther, superior of the Ursuline monastery in Quebec, had been captured and raised by the Abenaki. Even when she had a chance to return to her family, she declined, wishing to stay in Quebec to continue her ministry.

The Ursuline Convent, founded in Quebec in 1639, was the first of its Order in North America. The superior of the new foundation was Mère Marie Guyart de l'Incarnation.

General Louis-Joseph, Marquis de Montcalm, French commander of the forces aligned against the British at Quebec.

General James Wolfe, who along with General Amherst had taken Fortress Louisbourg for the British, next set his sights on Quebec.

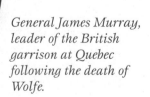

General James Murray, leader of the British garrison at Quebec following the death of Wolfe.

French ships were floated toward the British fleet and set afire in an attempt to burn the British vessels. The blazing ships were towed ashore and the British fleet remained unharmed.

Soldiers from Fraser's Highlanders, one of three highland regiments in the French and Indian War, and the only Scottish regiment to fight with the British troops on the Plains of Abraham.

September 13, 1759: British soldiers make the perilous climb from the river to face the French troops on the Plains of Abraham.

General Wolfe took three gunshots and died during the battle.

Left: General Montcalm directing his troops against a British attack.

Lower: In this rather romanticized painting, General Montcalm is shown dying a day after the battle, as a result of the serious wounds he had suffered.

Much of the upper town and lower town were badly damaged from the heavy shelling they received during the siege of Quebec.

The effects of the bombardment by the British are shown in the engravings from drawings made on the spot by Richard Short

Church of Notre Dame des Victoires & neighboring buildings

The ruins of Notre-Dame-des-Victoires and neighbouring buildings.

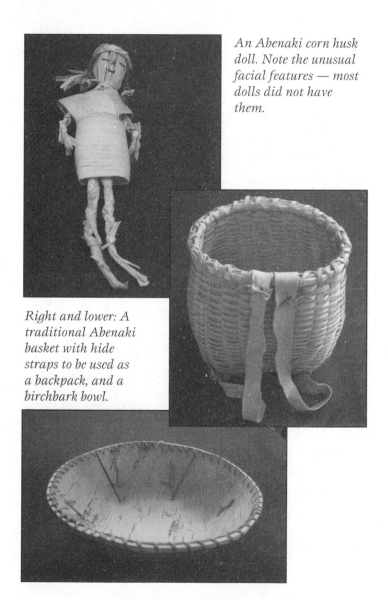

An Abenaki corn husk doll. Note the unusual facial features — most dolls did not have them.

Right and lower: A traditional Abenaki basket with hide straps to be used as a backpack, and a birchbark bowl.

Glossary: French

aigre-doux: bittersweet

après midi: afternooon

armoire: cupboard or wardrobe

avant l'aurore: before dawn

bâton: stick or staff

cajeux: rafts made of logs piled up and crossing at right angles

chemise: long "dress" made of light material and worn under other garments

cochon: pig

compote: stewed fruit

détachement: a military unit sent on special assignment

drôle: dryly amusing

eau de vie: brandy from France

Les Écossais: the Scottish

enceinte: pregnant

fichu: scarf

forgeron: blacksmith

les gens sans culottes: the Canadian nickname given to the Scots, meaning "men without pants"

Guignolée: the custom of going to visit relatives to wish them a happy New Year

hôpital: hospital

lapin: rabbit
le bon Dieu: merciful God
Marines: colonial regulars
mouchoir: handkerchief
pendant la nuit: night
pensionnaires: boarding students
pieds du roi: unit of measurement
pigeons de passage: wild migratory pigeons
plus tard: later
porte-crayon: a holder for graphite (an early
  version of the pencil)
potager: kitchen garden or vegetable garden
ragoût: stew
respectable: respectable
salut: informal greeting
souvenir: keepsake or memento
stupide: stupid/idiotic
tard: later
tard le soir: late at night
tarte: pie
tôt: early in the morning
tourtière: meat pie

Glossary: Abenaki

Alnanbal: Abenaki

anhahkoganal: woven mat

Chegual or *Chegwal*: frog

Jigenaz: hawthorn

Kwai: Hello or Greetings

mategwas or *matgwas*: rabbit

Miguen: feather

Toni kd'allowzin? or *Tôni Kd'wôlôwzi?*: Are you well? or How are you?

wigwedi or *wikwti*: lynx

(The alternate spellings are from the Odanak Abenaki, who live near what once was the St. Francis Mission.)

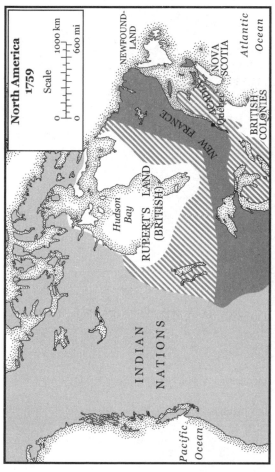

During the first half of the eighteenth century, the British tried to challenge the French for control of areas bordering New France (the striped areas on the map above). The French had a strong trading presence in these areas, and even established settlements as far west as Detroit and present-day Illinois. First Nations people, of course, lived across the whole of North America.

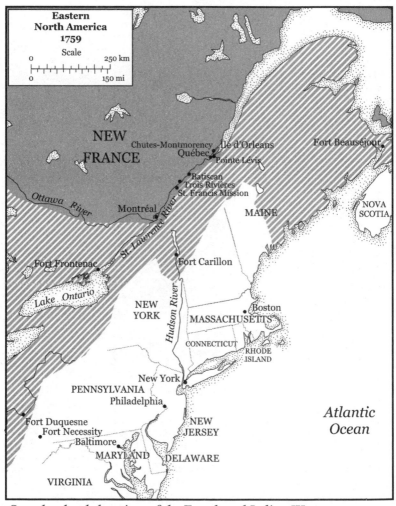

Some key battle locations of the French and Indian War.

Acknowledgments

Grateful acknowledgment is made for permission to reprint the following:

Cover Portrait: Detail, adapted, from *Emergence* by Karen Noles. Cover background: Detail, lightened, from *Mort de Montcalm* by Desfontaines. Library and Archives Canada, C-003759, The Source: R.W. Reford Estate, Montreal, Quebec.

Page 187: *First Ursuline Nuns with Indian Pupils at Quebec, Quebec* by Lawrence R. Batchelor. Library and Archives Canada, C-010520.

Page 188: *Ursuline Convent, Quebec, Québec* by James Pattison Cockburn. Library and Archives Canada, C-150519, Peter Winkworth Collection of Canadiana.

Page 189 (upper): *Louis-Joseph, Marquis de Montcalm* by Antoine Louis Francois Sergent. Library and Archives Canada, C-014342.

Page 189 (centre): *Portrait of James Wolfe, ca. 1749* by Joseph Highmore. Library and Archives Canada, C-003916.

Page 189 (lower): *James Murray, ca. 1770.* Library and Archives Canada, C-002834

Page 190: *The Defeat of the French Fireships Attacking the British Fleet at Anchor before Quebec, 28 June 1759, Quebec* by Dominic Serres/Samuel Scott. Library and Archives Canada, C-004291.

Page 191: *78th Regiment of Foot Guards: Fraser's Highlanders 1759* by Frederick M. Milner. Library and Archives Canada, C-005731, Bathurst and Milner Collection.

Page 192: *A View of the Taking of Québec, September 13th, 1759, Québec, Québec.* Library and Archives Canada, C-041757, W.H. Coverdale Collection of Canadiana.

Page 193: *The Death of General Wolfe, Québec* by Benjamin West; engraver William Woollett. Library and Archives Canada, C-041187, W. H. Coverdale Collection of Canadiana.

Page 194 (upper): *Montcalm leading his troops at Plains of Abraham, Quebec,* by C. W. Jefferys. Library and Archives Canada, C-073720.

Page 194 (lower): *Mort de Montcalm* by Desfontaines. Library and Archives Canada, C-003759, The Source: R.W. Reford Estate, Montreal, Quebec.

Page 195: *Ruins of Quebec after the Siege of 1759, Quebec* by C. W. Jefferys. Library and Archives Canada, C-070317.

Page 196: *Ruins of Quebec after the Siege of 1759, Quebec* by C. W. Jefferys. Library and Archives Canada, C-070318.

Page 197: Abenaki corn husk doll, basket and bowl, courtesy of the Odanak Reserve Museum.

Pages 201 and 202: Maps by Paul Heersink/Paperglyphs. Map data © 1999 Government of Canada with permission from Natural Resources Canada.

Acknowledgments: My thanks to Barbara Hehner for her careful checking of the manuscript, as well as Andrew Gallup, historian, writer and co-conspirator in re-enacting, for the same thoughtful work. My appreciation to Charlotte Picard and her husband John Ashley Sheltus, upon whom I based the characters of Mme Claire and Lieutenant Stewart. And as always, my thanks to my husband Bill for his endless patience and support.

*For Jeanette Murray-Pastorius, who has stood
at Culloden and who will never forget
who has gone before her.*

About the Author

An avid re-enactor, Maxine Trottier seems as at home in eighteenth-century Louisbourg as she does in twenty-first-century Ontario. Her mother's family has been in Canada since the seventeenth century. It was while researching her previous Dear Canada book, *Alone in an Untamed Land: The* Filles du Roi *Diary of Hélène St. Onge*, that Maxine made an intriguing disovery: the wife of one of her own ancestors was actually a *fille du roi* herself. Another of Maxine's ancestors married Marguerite Ouabankikove of the Miami tribe, the sister of chief Le Pied Froid, so Maxine has both European and First Nations ancestry.

Maxine is a frequent visitor to schools, where she is as likely to show up with quill pens, an inkpot and a tomahawk as with her books. In the summer she can frequently be found on a battlefield, re-enacting one of the key conflicts of the French and Indian War. She is part of a unit called *Le Détachement*, whose members portray militia and family members' lifestyles during the French and Indian War. "My family fought in that war," she says, "and so this story has great personal meaning for me. As a re-enactor, I have spent time at many of the sites mentioned in this book. To walk the dark hallways of Fort Niagara with a lantern in my hand, to look out from the King's Bastion in Louisbourg and imagine the British Navy's approach, to stand in the foggy meadow at Fort Necessity where the French and Indian War began . . . these are the sort of experiences that fuel a writer's imagination and, in doing so, keep history from seeming dry and dusty. Because it isn't. Geneviève's story, although a work of fiction, is the tale of people who stood bravely against tremendous odds for what they believed. And *that* has always been the story of Canada."

Maxine says that researching the facts and details for *The Death of My Country* presented interesting and sometimes frustrating challenges. "Historians differed on such things as how many men were in each army or how many were aboard the Royal Navy vessels. Even the journals of Lieutenant John Knox, and the letters and papers of French and British officers, varied in terms of what was seen and what happened." This made the research complicated, since it was often a case of deciding who was "most right." When writing about a historical event, each writer would have had a different agenda. Some men were making reports to their superiors; some, like Knox, were writing memoirs that they planned to have published. "I gathered as much information as possible and then set about shaping it into what I felt was the most correct information. Believe me, it was one of those times when I wished time travel were possible, so that I could have seen the story first-hand."

Maxine Trottier's first Dear Canada, *Alone in an Untamed Land, the* Filles du Roi *Diary of Hélène St. Onge,* was nominated for both the 2004 Silver Birch Award and the 2005 Hackmatack Award. Maxine is an award-winning writer of numerous books for young people, including the entire Scholastic Biographies series (*Canadian Artists, Canadian Explorers, Canadian Greats, Canadian Inventors, Canadian Leaders, Canadian Pioneers, Canadian Stars*), as well as *Claire's Gift* (winner of the Mr. Christie's Book Award), *Laura: A Childhood Tale of Laura Secord*, the *Circle of Silver Chronicles* (whose initial book was nominated for the CLA Book of the Year Award), and *The Tiny Kite of Eddie Wing* (winner of the CLA Book of the Year Award).

All rights reserved. Published by Scholastic Canada Ltd.
SCHOLASTIC and DEAR CANADA and logos are trademarks
and/or registered trademarks of Scholastic Inc.

Library and Archives Canada Cataloguing in Publication

Trottier, Maxine
The death of my country : the Plains of Abraham diary of Geneviève
Aubuchon / by Maxine Trottier.

(Dear Canada)

ISBN 0-439-96762-7

1. Abenaki Indians--Juvenile fiction. 2. Plains of Abraham, Battle of the,
Québec, Québec, 1759--Juvenile fiction. I. Title. II. Series.

PS8589.R685D42 2005   jC813'.54   C2005-900594-7

6 5 4 3 2 1   Printed in Canada   05 06 07 08 09

The display type was set in Poliphilus MT RegularSC.
The text was set in Esprit Book.

❧

Printed in Canada
First printing June 2005

❧

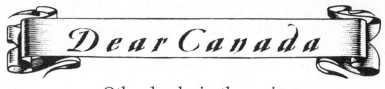
Dear Canada

Other books in the series:

A Prairie as Wide as the Sea
The Immigrant Diary of Ivy Weatherall
by Sarah Ellis

Orphan at My Door
The Home Child Diary of Victoria Cope
by Jean Little

With Nothing But Our Courage
The Loyalist Diary of Mary MacDonald
by Karleen Bradford

Footsteps in the Snow
The Red River Diary of Isobel Scott
by Carol Matas

A Ribbon of Shining Steel
The Railway Diary of Kate Cameron
by Julie Lawson

Whispers of War
The War of 1812 Diary of Susanna Merritt
by Kit Pearson